MAGAZINE

Tin House

Volume 19, Number 2

"Are people's lives so bankrupt they sit at home watching things they already did?"

—GEORGE CARLIN

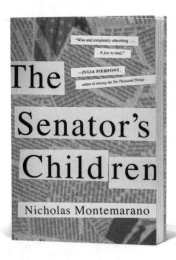
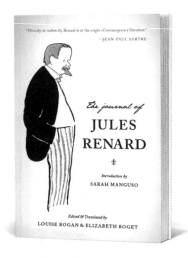

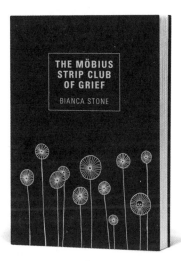

FREEBIRD
by Jon Raymond

** Now Out in Paperback **

"*Freebird* is such a timely book, considering the deep divisions between right and left. A new classic for the collapsing political landscape of America."

—KIM GORDON, author of *Girl in a Band*

"[*Freebird* is] the rare work of fiction that feels more timely with each passing moment."

—*Seattle Weekly*

"Thanks to Raymond's loose, masterful style, *Freebird* is an arm wrestling match between hilarity and heartbreak."

—*Interview*

"A binge-worthy novel, lightly satirical and compulsively readable."

—*Shelf Awareness*

THE MÖBIUS STRIP CLUB OF GRIEF
poetry by Bianca Stone

The Möbius Strip Club of Grief is a collection of poems that take place in a burlesque purgatory where the living pay—dearly, with both money and conscience—to watch the dead perform scandalous acts otherwise unseen.

"Bianca Stone's lyricism outright rejects the Wordsworthian definition, 'emotion recollected in tranquility'; there is nothing tranquil about these poems or the state in which they were written. Grief, loss, and disappointment are transferred to a landscape of wild objects and associations. We are propelled along by abrupt changes in perspective and dimension. Bianca Stone is a brilliant transcriber of her generation's emerging pathology and sensibility."

—JOHN ASHBERY

Available January 2018   **Available February 2018**

MFA and BFA
Portland State University

Fiction | Nonfiction | Poetry

Diana Abu-Jaber

John Beer

Paul Collins

Michele Glazer

Janice Lee

Gabriel Urza

Leni Zumas

James B. Norman, *The Portland Bridge Book*

Announcing for 2018

TIN HOUSE WRITER-IN-RESIDENCE: Audrey Petty

TIN HOUSE MASTERCLASS AND VISITING WRITER: John Edgar Wideman

www.pdx.edu/creativewriting

MFA application deadline for Fall 2018: January 15, 2018

 Portland State
UNIVERSITY

Tin House

MAGAZINE

EDITOR IN CHIEF / PUBLISHER
Win McCormack

EDITOR	Rob Spillman
DEPUTY PUBLISHER	Holly MacArthur
ART DIRECTOR	Diane Chonette
MANAGING EDITOR	Cheston Knapp
EXECUTIVE EDITOR	Michelle Wildgen
POETRY EDITOR	Camille T. Dungy
EDITOR-AT-LARGE	Elissa Schappell
PARIS EDITOR	Heather Hartley
ASSOCIATE EDITOR	Emma Komlos-Hrobsky
ASSISTANT EDITOR	Thomas Ross
COPY EDITOR	Meg Storey
SENIOR DESIGNER	Jakob Vala

CONTRIBUTING EDITORS: Dorothy Allison, Steve Almond, Aimee Bender, Charles D'Ambrosio, Natalie Diaz, Anthony Doerr, Nick Flynn, Matthea Harvey, Jeanne McCulloch, Rick Moody, Maggie Nelson, Whitney Otto, D. A. Powell, Jon Raymond, Helen Schulman, Jim Shepard, Karen Shepard

INTERNS: Rawz Addison, Enma Elias, Miriam Alexander-Kumaradoss, Jake Bartman, Cathryn Rose, Meritt Salathe

READERS: Leslie Marie Aguilar, William Clifford, Selin Gökçesu, Paris Gravely, Todd Gray, Lisa Grgas, Dahlia Grossman-Heinz, Carol Keeley, Louise Wareham Leonard, Su-Yee Lin, Maria Lioutai, Alyssa Persons, Sean Quinn, Lauren Roberts, Gordon Smith, Jennifer Taylor, J. R. Toriseva, Lin Woolman, Charlotte Wyatt

Tin House Magazine (ISSN 1541-521X) is published quarterly by McCormack Communications LLC, 2601 Northwest Thurman Street, Portland, OR 97210. Vol. 19, No. 2, Winter 2017. Printed by Versa Press, Inc. Send submissions (with SASE) to Tin House, P.O. Box 10500, Portland, OR 97296-0500. ©2017 McCormack Communications LLC. All rights reserved. No part of this publication may be reproduced, stored in a retrieval system, or transmitted in any form or by any means, electronic, mechanical, photocopying, recording, or otherwise, without the prior written permission of McCormack Communications LLC. Visit our Web site at **www.tinhouse.com**.

Basic subscription price: one year, $50.00. For subscription requests, write to P.O. Box 469049, Escondido, CA 92046-9049, or e-mail tinhouse@pcspublink.com, or call 1-800-786-3424. Circulation management by Circulation Specialists, Inc.

Periodicals postage paid at Portland, OR 97210 and additional mailing offices.

Postmaster: Send address changes to Tin House Magazine, P.O. Box 469049, Escondido, CA 92046-9049.

Newsstand distribution through Disticor Magazine Distribution Services (disticor.com). If you are a retailer and would like to order Tin House, call 905-619-6565, fax 905-619-2903, or e-mail Melanie Raucci at mraucci@disticor.com. For trade copies, contact W. W. Norton & Company at 800-233-4830.

At editorial meetings we often debate whether a piece contains "productive ambiguity," a term usually associated with mathematics, science, and philosophy. There's a fine line between being evocative and being obscure, between inviting the reader along for the journey and taking a reader for a ride to nowhere. The US is now run by a reckless and unpredictable madman, so day-to-day reality can feel like the ultimate unproductive ambiguity. It can be a struggle to give ourselves over to art, which is by its fundamental nature open to interpretation. Yet at the same time I've noticed a deep hunger for untidy creations, for a dream logic that somehow makes more sense than the hard, clinical takes on our permanent state of rage and resentment. In her short story "The Wolves," Kseniya Melnik blends Russian fairy tales with Stalin-era paranoia to bring us closer to the feeling of Russian history while at the same time shining light on the dark underpinnings of our current moment. In an excerpt from her forthcoming novel, *Red Clocks*, Leni Zumas gives us a world where abortion has been outlawed, creating a state that feels like a lucid dream. In this issue we have more poetry than usual, as it seems contemporary poets are especially attuned to the productive ambiguity frequency and now is one of those zeitgeist moments when we most need them. Paisley Rekdal, in her poem "Marsyas," writes that Apollo "never understands what he plays, / knowing only how his hand / trembles over the plucked muscle: / adding, he thinks, something lower to the notes, / something sweeter, and infinitely strange." We hope the work here plucks at something sweeter, and infinitely strange, and that the entire issue feels productively ambiguous. We're happy to have you on the journey with us.

CONTENTS

ISSUE #74 / WINTER READING

Fiction

Poetry

Nonfiction

The Wolves

Kseniya Melnik

It was nine o'clock on a balmy summer evening when Masha stepped off the last bus to Shelkovskaya, a village in Chechnya. The year was 1938, the second year of what is now known as Yezhovshchina, the bloodiest phase of the Great Purge named in honor of Nikolai Yezhov, the head of the Soviet secret police. Historians from all around the world still argue about the number of unnatural deaths from those two years alone—the upper estimate surpassing a million. But Masha did not know it then. And even if she had, this wouldn't have been her main concern. She was a girl, a carefree college student until a week ago, when she found out that she was accidentally, unfortunately, unhappily pregnant.

Although she was afraid of the long journey ahead, she believed that if she squeezed her mother's small, silky hand, and if she watched her father's coarse yellow eyebrows wiggle in laughter, and after she spent one night sleeping with her two sisters in their bedroom—the same room where the great Russian writer Mikhail Lermontov had once spent the night a hundred years prior—her thoughts and feelings would gain proper balance. She would know what to do.

Masha watched the bright windows of the sputtering bus until it disappeared around the turn. The two men in workers' caps and oil-splattered overalls who had gotten off with her at Shelkovskaya were also looking after the bus. Once it was out of view, they turned and regarded her with weary, disappointed expressions—or so it appeared to Masha. They bowed, spun on their heels like soldiers, and hurried off toward their village.

An invisible crow cawed.

Aside from the red First of May banner, which, strangely, still hung from the side of a brick house near the bus stop though it was already July, the village was gray, sinking into twilight. The cows and horses dream-walked in the purple field nearby, knee-deep in fog. In seconds, the backs of the men, too, turned gray, then disappeared. But why only two of them today, Masha wondered. Usually, a crowd of workers disembarked at Shelkovskaya in the evenings. At any rate, they were home now. Masha, on the other hand, had to walk sixteen kilometers on a forest trail to reach Paraboch, the village where her father worked as the director of the Red Star forestry service.

She stood under the solitary light post, hoping that a fellow traveler to Paraboch would appear. The trees seemed swollen and heavy, as if they'd hoarded darkness all day, sucking it up from the rich black soil through the roots and into their branches, and would shoot it into the sky at any moment. The air was still warm and sweet, though she could see no flowering trees. The skin over her ribs and under her breasts began to itch.

This very minute her boyfriend, Sasha, could be climbing the stairs to the two-room apartment Masha shared with four classmates from the university to ask if she wanted to go dancing to the brass band in the park. She hadn't told him that she

Masha froze, then walked faster. The howls came as if from a great distance.

urgently needed to see her parents. He would've accompanied her. He would've been happy to sleep on the threadbare couch that had traveled with her family from Ukraine to Chechnya.

Masha couldn't wait any longer. She was nauseated yet hungry. She entered the forest, which, despite the full moon in the lilac sky, felt to her like a big house with curtains drawn over all the windows. She scolded herself for forgetting the flashlight. A nightingale trilled on every branch, but there was something mechanical about those trills. Someone called out insistently and close. After a few airless seconds, she turned around. No one. It must've been a stray jay. Jays always sounded as if they were in trouble. And then Masha heard it. A plaintive siren—a howl. Another howl. Two howls in a duet. Three howls.

Wolves.

Masha froze, then walked faster. The howls came as if from a great distance. Still she was afraid. She had become a spoiled city girl, her father would say, she had forgotten with whom she shared the forest. Bears, boars, deer, wolves.

The bushes jolted. A harmless fox, maybe, or a weasel. To scare them, she opened her dry mouth and shrieked a couplet from an old Ukrainian lullaby her mother used to sing to her and her sisters before bed. The trees cringed, stuffing their ears with leaves.

They had met at a dance in the city park three months earlier, Sasha and Masha, and their friends immediately declared them a perfect match. They were both at the top of their respective classes in Grozny, she at the newly founded Teacher Training College and he at the Higher Technical School for Petroleum Studies. They were musically inclined: she sang in the student choir and he was a drummer in a band. Even their names rhymed. When Sasha first saw Masha in the park, the family story goes, he promptly abandoned the bandstand and asked her to dance to the tune that seemed to go on just fine without his drumming. From that day on he didn't let go of her. And she barely noticed how quickly her Grozny—the steps to the library, the quiet alley behind the movie theater, even the tram ride to her home— became their Grozny. Sasha had very gallantly, very stealthily, invaded and occupied the topography of her surroundings, and, two months ago, she had let him infiltrate her body.

> She couldn't see or hear the wolves; they were stealthy on the hunt.

Yet, she couldn't get rid of the feeling that, if only she tried hard enough, she could unhear the verdict, unattend the event, reel back the unspooling time. She could march on into the future—the way it happened with Egor, a schoolmate whom she'd spurned in seventh grade: when she heard the previous year that he had drowned on a fishing trip, she felt guilty—as if he had died shouting her name—then, a week or two later, the shock wore off, the grief retreated, and Egor sunk back to the dark bottom of her memory well, bobbing up as rarely as before. Time took care of everything. But did she love Sasha, she had wondered ever since she found out that she was pregnant, the way Egor had loved her?

Masha hadn't heard any more howling; as a forester's daughter she knew that the wolves didn't howl while on a hunt. But they were close now. She felt them with the tips of her ears. She walked faster still, while little stones and twigs attacked her toes, exposed in her summer sandals.

What a stupid girl she really was, to let this happen. And yet, she wasn't the first one. In the dormitory bathroom, under the cover of shower steam, she'd heard whispers of an old Chechen woman at an aul south of Grozny who made special black tea. She'd also heard that, if drunk too late, it would kill both the girl and the thing growing inside her.

Or—if Sasha really meant the things he'd whispered into her blotchy neck under the acacia's shadow—there was still time to get married quickly. People would not be surprised at the blessing bestowed on a young couple so in love and in a hurry to start their lives. Many years later, Masha could tell her firstborn about how she was pursued by wolves through the forest and survived. Her firstborn would think that his mother was from some ancient time of fairy tales, and Masha would laugh and tell him that such a thing could happen anywhere, anytime, even now.

And, like in a fairy tale, she suddenly remembered that somewhere close stood the cabin of the forester responsible for this sector. She knew she must find it before the wolves snatched her and dragged her into the darkness.

Masha raced through the darkness. She couldn't see or hear the wolves; they were stealthy on the hunt. But she could smell the dead squirrels on their short breath.

The cabin sprang up as if it had been lying in wait. The forester's dogs— three dirty brown mutts—exploded with barking. Masha threw open the gate. The shed stirred with bigger animals: a spotted cow, mauve pigs, a white horse glowing in the moonlight like a ghost. Here, the cool forest air was laced with the smell of manure.

Masha pounded on the wooden door. The mutts tore their throats with barks, but kept their distance from her. She put her ear to the door: Were those footsteps? Was that a bump? A clink of glass, a ring of metal?

"Help me! Hide me from the wolves!" she screamed into the door. She darted to one of the curtained windows and banged on the dirty glass.

The door creaked open, and she was struck by the sharp smell of rotting peaches. Before her stood a man with a pale, frightened face. He was dressed as if for a long journey north—in a wool coat and an *ushanka* hat, a lumpy scarf wrapped tight around his neck. He clutched a cracked leather traveling bag. The purple veins on his temples bulged like scars.

She knew this man, Masha realized: Stepan Dmitrievich. He had been a frequent guest at her father's house in Paraboch—where she was now headed—the year she turned twelve. Her parents told her that he had fled the Holodomor famine in Ukraine, where a long time before then their families had been neighbors.

That whole year Masha had a crush on Stepan Dmitrievich. She even thought he resembled young Lermontov, the great Russian writer who had a hundred years prior spent the night in their big old wooden house in Paraboch. Then one day Stepan Dmitrievich disappeared. She was shocked to learn that he presently worked for her father. She had seen him neither at the forestry directorate, which occupied the lower part of the house, nor at her parents' apartment, which occupied the upper part of it. Perhaps he'd been walking through the rooms all these years subtly transformed, a shadow of himself. Perhaps she hadn't been recognizing him.

He now wore thin-wired round glasses. Was that it?

Stepan Dmitrievich looked her over as if he'd never seen her before: her white summer dress, her worn sandals full of moss and twigs, her satchel, her new watch—a present from Sasha.

"It's me, Masha! Masha from Paraboch. I—"

His gaze steeled, then hollowed. He slapped Masha on the cheek.

"The wolves—" she began to say, tears salting her throat.

The brown mutts yowled into the blackness of the forest.

His soul rushed back into him; his face flushed red.

"I apologize," Stepan Dmitrievich mumbled. He stepped back, looking at his shoes, then at his bag. He was shorter now, Masha noticed. "I apologize. I apologize."

"I am Masha," she said. "Masha Korol." She quickly wiped her eyes with the backs of her hands.

He stepped aside, and Masha dashed into the cabin. Slowly, he closed the door. Slowly, he set the bag down, took off his hat, unknotted his scarf—his neck was purple, glistening with sweat—and removed his winter coat. He folded everything into an ancient wooden trunk, then paused and pulled it all out again. He piled his winter clothes on top of the trunk.

"I'm sorry to disturb you, Stepan Dmitrievich. I am on my way to Paraboch, to my parents. You remember my parents, don't you? Can I wait here till the wolves are gone? I beg you."

Why? Why did he slap her? Or did she imagine it?

She tried to swallow her nausea, her self-pity.

His onion skin was cut with creases around his blue eyes, which, in turn, had a look both blank and startled, like the old gelatin prints where people's pupils burn with cold fire. His wavy hair was still completely black.

He turned to Masha, tears pooling inside his concave cheeks. "Only the *leshy* and wood goblins wander the forest at night, knocking on innocent doors."

"I'm sorry I scared you."

"You didn't scare me, Masha!" Stepan Dmitrievich took a deep breath. He must have recognized her at last.

"I know I shouldn't have left Grozny so late, I shouldn't have been walking alone."

"Yes. Well, that can hardly be avoided these days. *Nu*, sit down, be a guest."

"I'm sorry, I'm so sorry."

Masha perched on one of the stools at the big rough-hewn table by the window. But the stool wasn't used to a stranger's bony backside and immediately threw her off with its sharp edge. She bruised her coccyx as she landed on the floor.

"Be careful. Everything is wobbly here, barely holding itself together," Stepan Dmitrievich said. He remained standing, turned slightly away from her. His arms, limp along his seams, appeared prosthetic. He must be embarrassed by his tears, waiting for them to dry, she thought. She got up, rubbing her back, and sat down on the other stool. She held on to the table.

> Confused, Masha put her hand on her gurgling stomach and looked around.

"Who'd you think was at the door, Stepan Dmitrievich? Whom were you waiting for?"

"Catch your breath while I check on the animals." He scurried out of the cabin.

Confused, Masha put her hand on her gurgling stomach and looked around.

The giant Russian oven, a whitewashed brick mausoleum, took up most of the one-room cabin. A metal door shut up the oven's hearth, a black tongue of coal smeared above it, as if something had escaped from there in a blast of fire. The corner of a checkered afghan peeked out from beneath the curtains that concealed the sleeping nook on top of the oven. Some firewood huddled under a bench in the corner. A large metal-frame bed was stripped of all bedding. A portrait of Stalin and two hunting rifles hung on the wall. A lamp, the sole source of light in the cabin, stood on the table. A metal bucket with water and a cupboard with cookware and dishes placed at even distances from each other completed the rustic ensemble.

There wasn't a single photograph, book, or newspaper. Masha felt as if she were sitting inside a diorama at the museum.

And didn't Stepan Dmitrievich have a wife, the wife Masha had been so jealous of at twelve? She had a hazy memory of a small woman with short brown hair and a big nose that didn't make her ugly. Mostly, Masha remembered being mortified whenever her mother reminisced in the company of Stepan Dmitrievich and his wife how, back in Ukraine, Stepan Dmitrievich would put baby Masha on his knees and bounce her "over the hassocks and the hillocks," and then he would open his legs and she would fall as if into a pit, laughing hysterically. Masha hadn't wanted to know any personal details about him then; she preferred that he live in her fantasies. She didn't even ask if her parents knew why he'd disappeared.

> She was ravenous, despite the smell of rotting peaches, despite her nausea.

Many years later she would learn that he had been arrested as a kulak, and served an eight-year sentence. She would understand that her father had taken a huge risk hiring him and had done a huge favor to Stepan Dmitrievich, who—carrying the documents of an ex-prisoner—would have had trouble finding decent employment. Along with millions who managed to remain on the periphery of purges and repressions, she would attempt to absorb the statistics of suffering and she would find it impossible, sometimes even unnecessary. But, for now, Masha sat in the cabin hungry, nauseated, hurt by the unjust slap, and, most of all, relieved that she had escaped from the wolves.

Stepan Dmitrievich returned in a brighter mood. He sat down on the rebellious stool, which only creaked under his sudden charm, and trained his bespectacled gaze at her. Masha's blood pushed against her stomach. She looked away. The reflection of his drawn face in the curves of the golden samovar, which she hadn't noticed before, appeared like a sketch someone had tried to erase but only managed to smudge.

He seized her hand, slipped down her clammy skin, and shook her fingers.

"Forgive me, Mashenka. Really forgive me for what I did earlier. I thought it wouldn't be you."

"Whom did you think it would be?" she said, warmth spreading outward from her diaphragm.

"Whom? The wolves!" He broke out in tinny laughter.

She stared at him until a visual memory—something from her childhood—floated up to the surface of his skin and softened it.

Stepan Dmitrievich got up and sprang toward the cupboard. Masha was unnerved to watch him just barely miss the steps of his old self. He produced a bottle of vodka and put it on the table.

"Always make sure you have enough vodka for your night guests," he exclaimed, beaming wildly now, showing his crooked, bluish teeth. "Let's drink to our narrow escape!"

Masha covered her stomach with her hand. Then, paranoid, she threw her hand off. Stepan Dmitrievich grabbed two glasses from the cupboard and filled them to the brim. He took one and pushed the other toward Masha.

"I'd rather have some tea," she said. She was ravenous, despite the smell of rotting peaches, despite her nausea. "I feel sick after vodka." She looked toward the oven. The coal tongue mocked her, the two small holes—one a square and the other a half-moon—smirked. But she couldn't ask for food; she was struck dumb with the shyness of a kid.

"Drink, Masha, drink. You never know when it will be your last glass." Stepan Dmitrievich sat back down.

"Or your last cup of tea," she tried to joke as he brought his glass to hers and clinked it.

Masha took a small sip so as not to offend him. He shook his head and emptied both glasses to the last drop.

"How are you liking a student's life, then? It must be so exciting to be in the city after your father hid you girls in the forest for so long, like little secret princesses." Stepan Dmitrievich smiled with his silverish eyes.

"I really like living in Grozny," Masha said.

He nodded, but it seemed to Masha that he was thinking about something else entirely.

"Remind me your subject."

"Russian Language and Literature."

"Ah yes, I remember. Whenever I came to visit your papa, you always hid behind a book. You never wanted to come out of your made-up little world. No point in even trying to start a game with you. Going to be a teacher?"

"Yes." She shifted under his stare and itched her arms.

"A noble profession, teaching." Stepan Dmitrievich became animated, jerking like a puppet on strings. "My mother always wanted to learn to read, but she was busy helping my father run the farm. Farming is backbreaking work. Every chick, every kid, every calf she tended to like her own child. Did you know that I grew up in a house as big as your father's? Both floors."

"No," she said. "And did you know that a hundred years ago Lermontov spent the night in my sisters' room?" She felt stupid for saying this, young.

"What Lermontov?"

"Lermontov. Whom you look like." She blushed. "The poet of the Caucasus. You don't know? *A Hero of Our Time*. Also, 'A little golden cloud spent the night on the breast of the behemoth cliff—'"

"*Nu da*, some hero of our time," Stepan Dmitrievich said. He poured another glass of vodka for himself and threw the liquid down his throat. The vodka lit up something in his stomach; he looked at her with new hunger: "You love poetry?"

She chuckled. "Of course."

"And your parents love poetry, don't they? I know."

"Doesn't everyone?"

He rubbed the grain of the table's wood with his right hand. His fingers were thin, with big, knotty joints. Two of the nails on his right hand were gone—one completely, exposing a spoon of hardened watermelon flesh, and another halfway.

"Who are your parents' favorite poets, I forgot—"

Masha didn't understand why Stepan Dmitrievich cared about her parents' preferences, not hers. She wanted to be older for him, more serious.

"Pushkin," she said.

"Everyone loves Pushkin." Stepan Dmitrievich's mouth was open, his lips glistened. "Who else?"

Masha thought back to all the books that had once stood on her parents' shelves and now lay hidden in their own ancient wooden trunk, the same books she remembered traveling with like family members from house to house during the many moves of her childhood.

"Fet, Nekrasov, Lermontov, of course."

"Of course, your Lermontov. Mendelstump?"

"Mandelstam? No, not him."

"Oh, yes, of course, never him. God forbid. What about this Gamalov?"

The gleaming white plates gawked at her with dumb innocence.

"You mean Gumilyov?" she whispered. "Don't you know—he, just like Mandelstam, is listed as an enemy of the people."

Maybe Stepan Dmitrievich hadn't heard from where he'd been all these years, Masha thought, though this was old news.

Stepan Dmitrievich nodded quickly and worked his thin lips, as if chewing. The white cups on the shelf wanted more; they had one handle of an ear each.

"My parents don't read much poetry these days," Masha said. "They only joke about Lermontov's ghost."

"What kind of joke?"

"How he haunts my sisters' room, not letting them sleep at night."

Stepan Dmitrievich groaned.

She looked toward the oven. It seemed to be growing hotter.

Though she was a smart university girl, she didn't understand what he wanted from her. Some part of her didn't even want to try.

> Though she was a smart university girl, she didn't understand what he wanted from her.

"So, how's the groom?"

Masha started. She had completely forgotten about Sasha.

"Your parents told me how dedicated Comrade Biryukov is to you."

"He's not my groom. He—"

Stepan Dmitrievich glanced toward the door. His dogs began to bark, then stopped abruptly, as though gagged.

"I didn't hear anything," Masha whispered.

He turned back to her, his face zapped clean of all expression. He took a breath. His features resettled. "And Sasha has already been recommended for the Party?" he said in a trembling voice.

"Yes." She didn't care about politics—no one in her family did—but she'd noted the extra dose of respect most people, including her parents, paid to Sasha.

"Excellent. Admirable. Marry him."

Masha's face flared. Could he have really sensed her condition the way foresters sensed disease in the trees and changes in insect populations, like the wolves sensed her fear?

A noise slipped from the oven. Or behind the oven. A mouse?

"Stepan Dmitrievich, if you're hungry, I can throw something together for you. You seem so alone here, so abandoned."

He chortled. "I may be abandoned, but I am certainly not alone." He glanced toward the wall where Stalin's portrait and the rifles hung. "The wolves are rabid this year. They've bred so much, you can't take a step without running into one."

"My father said that, too."

"Your father knows."

Stepan Dmitrievich poured more vodka into his glass. His right, bird-like shoulder stuck out higher than the left. The right side of his chest was ever so slightly concave, as if missing a bone or two. A pang of hunger dug under Masha's ribs; her head began to spin.

"Yes . . . time marches on. And now we have a new constitution," he said.

Masha nodded.

"And the first elections to the Supreme Soviet under the new constitution are to be held soon. What do your parents make of it?"

> She found she was physically unable to turn her thoughts toward her most pressing question.

"Of what?"

"The Supreme Soviet."

"I don't know."

"No, of course, you wouldn't know."

"I could ask Sasha—"

"Don't bother. My questions are too simplistic for him."

She could see that Stepan Dmitrievich was disappointed. She hated to have disappointed him.

He turned on the radio on the table and fiddled with the knobs. A tango came on, and a distracted expression returned to his face. He looked as though he hadn't slept in days.

"When you were a baby in that beautiful house of yours in Ukraine, I would dance with you," he said, staring at the thick window curtains. "I danced with you all the time. Even your father got jealous. You didn't cry in my arms."

Masha's body softened at these words, became heavier and more liquid somehow. She found she was physically unable to turn her thoughts toward her most pressing question. The lightbulb in the lamp fizzled and grew dimmer. She felt inexplicable tenderness toward Stepan Dmitrievich, a man who earlier in the night had slapped her.

He took off his wire-rimmed glasses and pressed his fists against his eyes. He downed his vodka. He no longer offered any to her. She felt as if she'd stepped off the careening train of time and was waiting at a station. Simultaneously, the creature inside her seemed to be growing not by days but by hours.

Weary sun tenderly bid farewell to the sea, sang the crooner on the radio. *In this hour you confessed that there is no love . . .*

"Would you like to dance?" Masha blurted out before her mind could stop her.

We are parting, I won't be angry . . . You and I are to blame for it.

Red-faced, Stepan Dmitrievich planted his feet between the beats, on top of her feet. His right hand swept across her back, up and down, up and down. His left hand clutched hers in a clammy grip. The room spun, as if she were the one who had drunk all that vodka. At last he threw her into a dip and, afraid to fall, she screamed.

The radio began to chirp the late news program. He lunged to shut it off. Dark patches spread in his armpits. The scar-veins on his neck glistened with sweat. He smiled at her wildly, as if he'd just jumped from a tall cliff and hadn't broken his legs. She still didn't understand what was happening. She still felt like a little girl.

"Stepan Dmitrievich, please, can you give me something to eat? I am starving," she finally confessed, fighting through her embarrassment.

"Ah, of course. How rude of me not to offer. I always keep something warm in my oven especially for my night visitors."

As he moved aside the metal door, the oven let out an angry, smoked-through sigh and reluctantly disgorged a big cast-iron pot. He took two immaculate plates off the shelf. One bolted out of his hand and shattered on the floor. He put the surviving plate on the table and began to gather the fragments of the broken plate with such speed and care as if they were diamonds. He refused Masha's offer of help, saying that she'd prick her fingers on the shards.

After crawling around on all fours to check that he had collected every last piece and, while he was at it, test the stability of some of the floorboards, Stepan Dmitrievich seemed satisfied. He brought over another plate, clutching it with both hands—one finger on his left hand was also missing a nail—and ladled some of the dark mass for Masha.

"Eat, Masha, and don't worry about anything. Morning is wiser than the night."

She put a chunk of meat into her mouth. It melted on her tongue. It was the most delicious stew she'd ever tried. She stared hard at each piece of the meat she ate, cradling it in the spoon. Happiness penetrated her body with insistent, quickening breath. She felt the baby eat the meat inside of her. It liked the meat. Her nausea retreated. Her skin quieted down, stopped listening.

"Where did you disappear, Stepan Dmitrievich? Eight years ago?"

Stepan Dmitrievich cocked his head to one side and smiled.

"Do you collect stamps, Masha? I used to love collecting stamps as a child. Have you seen any foreign stamps at your parents' house?"

"No," she said.

Stepan Dmitrievich looked crushed. The air in the cabin hung heavy. Masha looked toward the ceiling as if expecting to see actual soot clouds. She wiped the sweat off her forehead. Even though hunger had left her, she kept eating for strength.

"One of my sisters collects stamps. I think I've seen an unusual one in her album before. Are you interested in a trade?"

In the near darkness the oven winked at her with its crooked eyes.

"I *am* interested in a trade. Can you check what she has?"

"Of course."

He sighed. "It might still amount to nothing."

"I'll look hard, I promise. And thank you so much for saving me."

"No need to thank me. Your wolves I'd fight with my bare hands. The night is not over yet, but let's try to sleep."

She looked at the wall: the tight-lipped rifles seemed to have switched places with each other. "I think I should go home."

"You'll have to stay the night."

As if pushed by a cold hand, she sat down on the bare metal bed.

"Don't sit on that!"

Masha shot up, but her happiness stayed lodged in her throat.

"It's broken, it's not for you," Stepan Dmitrievich said slowly, as if already half asleep. "You can sleep with me on top of the oven. I don't take up much space these days, I turn into a little worm. Or you can stay up if you like. Sorry I don't have any great books to offer. None of your Lermontovs, and definitely no Gamalovs."

"I don't need them." Masha wanted to stop him from doing something, but she wasn't sure what. She wanted to keep talking; she wanted to keep swimming in the viscous air of the cabin, like in a hot bath.

Stepan Dmitrievich stood guard "for the wolves" while she went to the outhouse, distracting himself with a song, like she'd asked, because she was embarrassed to go to the bathroom so near him. Afterward, he poured cold water from the well over a metal bowl as Masha washed her hands and face. She did the same for him, flinching when she touched his bird-boned shoulder, when she stepped on his little foot.

He put his glasses on the table, climbed on top of the oven, and disappeared behind the curtain.

Masha sat at the table. She looked at her hands, her arms—several coarse black hairs had sprouted between the soft chick down she'd had since childhood. She scratched them until she drew blood.

Something began to scrape at the door.

"It's just my cat, Anton," Stepan Dmitrievich said from behind the curtain.

"Should I let him in?"

"No use. He'll be running in and out all night."

"He must be hungry."

"There are things for him to hunt in the forest. Come to bed, Masha."

And, as if hypnotized, Masha turned off the light and felt her way up the warm oven. She lay down on her side, facing away from Stepan Dmitrievich. The oven pressed against her ribs, pushing the sweet curtain of sleep away from her eyes. Anton stopped scratching. She waited for him to start again. And a few minutes or hours later, he resumed, more frantic.

She felt the baby eat the meat inside of her. It liked the meat. Her nausea retreated.

"Are you asleep?" Masha whispered.

Stepan Dmitrievich shuddered and threw his arm over her. Her whole body seemed to fall through the brick partition and into the oven's fiery belly, where witches were known to cook stray children for dinner. She could feel his elbow against her hip, the caps of his knees against her thighs. She could imagine him sliding his hand lower, lower. She could fathom turning to him in the hot darkness. Testing his birdlike shoulder, counting his cold ribs, waiting for his response to her secret, shameful, awkward, inopportune love. She wanted to. And this scared her more than the wolves, more than telling Sasha about the pregnancy, more than looking for the Chechen woman who made the black herb tea that could put her to sleep forever.

"Tell me a story," Masha whispered, her tongue a dead fish in her mouth. She wanted relief, comfort. She wanted to think of anything but her chaotic heart.

"With pleasure. Listen carefully then, my darling. Once upon a time—" And immediately, as if by the power of that magical incantation, she turned into a young child again. A secret door opened inside her mind, and she was pushed into a cozy room, a room where she would believe anything. He moved closer to her, rubbing his nail-less fingers against her palm. "Once upon a time there lived a beautiful young girl in one of the fairest cities of a big and mighty empire. She had three brothers, whom she adored and admired like no other. She could not imagine her life without them and sometimes missed them even at night, in her dreams, because they slept in different rooms at the ends of long hallways in their big wooden castle. They grew up in abundance and happiness, fighting only over the petty kinds of things children fight over during peaceful times.

> He could be her shelter from the wildness inside her and out in the world.

"Then came the Great War. The three brothers became officers and went to the front to fight for the czar. They fought bravely and became, one could say, the heroes of their time. The youngest brother was killed in the first month of the war. The entire fair city came out for his funeral. I was there, I saw their young sister in mourning, beautiful like a black bird except when she opened her mouth and cackled like a wounded crow. The other two brothers continued to fight even harder, with even more courage and abandon. When the mighty empire pulled out of the war because, it realized, it had a greater war to fight at home, the czar awarded the two older brothers three Crosses of Saint George each, and their names were engraved on the honorary wall in the Kremlin. But then the revolution came."

Masha had never heard of fairy tales about revolutions. The real revolution hadn't yet fallen deep enough into the black well in the forest from which all the fairy tales were drawn.

"The brothers escaped on the last ship leaving Crimea for Turkey. And where are they now? Their sister, who is all grown up and has raised her own happy family in abundance, claims not to know. France? Maybe Bulgaria. Maybe even America. Some people still remember them, you see."

Why was he telling her this? What was he asking? He was drunk; he was raving mad from spending so much time alone in a cabin where his own broken plates waited for the right moment to latch on to his throat.

"Half an army abroad, half an army disappeared. Too many valiant soldiers to keep track of, too many bereft sisters," Stepan Dmitrievich continued still. "But if the brothers were writing to their sister from abroad, from Europe, that could be very dangerous."

"Yes, very dangerous." Masha heard her voice echo flatly in the dark. Perhaps it was the walls that said this. Officers. Crosses of Saint George. France. She didn't want to know any of this. She knew of no one who had so many uncles. She wanted to hear another story, a real fairy tale this time.

"You are a bright girl, with a bright future. You must be vigilant," he said.

But, oh, it was too late, she wanted to tell him. She hadn't been vigilant, and soon she would be unable to hide the evidence under any of her dresses.

For the rest of the night, Masha lay pinned to the oven by Stepan Dmitrievich's arm, which grew heavier and heavier. Her mind was on fire, her body paralyzed. From time to time something hooted outside, something snorted with disdain in the shed. A crow cawed, and, for some reason, she thought of her mother, and how she had never seen her cry.

Though she heard no more howls, in the very black of the night, when she was still feverishly awake, she began to think the wolves were scraping at the door. Or was Sasha? Or the White officers, who had come in the night from France and Bulgaria and America to tell her something very important, something she didn't want to know? She didn't let them in. She sensed that Stepan Dmitrievich was awake too, watching her through his closed silver lids. The rifles on the wall clenched their teeth but didn't fire. The portrait of Stalin, however, had pronounced his final, silent verdict on her unpremeditated crimes.

In the morning, Stepan Dmitrievich lifted his arm and let her escape.

The forest was awash with golden light. It was a different, wholly new forest. Every joint in Masha's body ached. Her feet were pure ice. She ran toward Shelkovskaya station, toward Grozny, toward Sasha. She hoped the acacia tree hadn't yet shed its leaves and there was time yet to turn her blotchy neck toward Sasha's lips under its shade. He could be her shelter from the wildness inside her and out in the world.

A nightingale, exhausted by his night song, sat on a tree branch and watched the girl in the white dress stumble over the roots and crags on the forest trail. He had seen many such girls run into the forest before, and only a few of them had ever come out. The nightingale shook the morning dew from his feathers and flew higher and higher, his heart beating violently, past the crowns of the trees, toward the white yawning sun. From the top of the forest the nightingale saw the timber-processing buildings of the Red Star forestry huddled in the distance, the piles of cut trees, and rectangular batteries of trees stripped of leaves and bark—no longer recognized as trees. They had become lumber.

The nightingale rose higher still. There was Paraboch, much closer than it appeared in the misty distance, and on its main street stood the beautiful big house, and on its second floor was the comfortable apartment of Masha's parents, and in that apartment was the room where the great Russian writer Mikhail Lermontov had once spent the night a hundred years ago. In that room, Masha's young sisters still slept their child's sleep, dreaming of the cabin on chicken legs, the magic frog skin, and the milk river with fruit jelly shores. Farther away were the great mountains of the North Caucasus, and beyond them lay Georgia, Armenia, Turkey, and the rest of the blue world, where, borderlessly, the birds were limited in their flight by their strength and their hunger alone.

Masha never looked for foreign stamps in her sister's album. Mostly because she was busy with planning for her wedding and the arrival of her first child. But also—if someone had pressed her in the night for truth—out of blurry fear that she might find them. And then everything that was old and unspoken—and there were such things in every family, especially the ones who had moved so many times—would rise from the bottom of the cold, dark well and say its name, demand that its days and years be counted by the survivors, the descendants.

Not long after that night—she didn't know the exact date—Stepan Dmitrievich disappeared from her life for the third and final time. In the late '50s, when her son entered university and the country's murderous policies became public—when millions of people realized they had been dancing on the edge of a precipice—Masha came to believe that Stepan Dmitrievich had been rearrested, like so many former kulaks, and possibly shot.

She had cried many nights for him, and for herself, for her vague suspicion that there had been something off about her encounter with Stepan Dmitrievich that night had finally coalesced into a stark realization: Stepan Dmitrievich, sensing danger, had been probing for any evidence with which to inform on Masha's family—a common way, she now knew, for former prisoners to preempt a rearrest, to prove they had decisively transformed into good Soviet patriots.

She never knew exactly how close she had brought her family to danger with her idle talk, her stupidity, her willful ignorance. It could have been death. It could have been nothing.

A few more years later, when Masha's grandson started happily shouting his first words, she learned that Stepan Dmitrievich's story had been no fable, after all. Her mother had three brothers once, White officers in the last czar's army. The youngest one was killed, and the other two had fled Russia on the last ship from Crimea, just like Stepan Dmitrievich had said all those years ago. One settled in Bulgaria and another in France, in Paris. Both brothers wrote to their sister when it was considered safe. The Bulgarian brother returned to Russia in the '60s to reunite with his sister after a forty-year absence. And the French brother—well, like so many others, he was forever lost to history and geography.

Now, Masha, who is more than ninety, has told the story of that night for the first time—to her great-granddaughter, who wants to be a writer, who's been worming her way into Masha's decaying memories to find meaning in the past. She finds it more narratively interesting than the present.

> She never knew exactly how close she had brought her family to danger with her idle talk, her stupidity.

"You gained political consciousness that night, right? You lost your innocence, you stopped being in denial. You came out of the cabin changed, reborn," the quick-witted great-granddaughter insists. "The epiphany was twofold: you realized that you didn't love Sasha/loved Stepan Dmitrievich, and that the pregnancy might not have been the biggest problem for you and your family. Our family."

Masha snorts, baring her toothless gums. How sharp, how wolfish is the girl's hindsight.

"But does it still feel real? Does it feel like it happened to you?" the girl asks.

"After all these years, it didn't happen to me, it happened to someone else."

"So, you decided to keep the baby and marry Great-grandpa Sasha to hedge the bets against a possible arrest? I mean, I think you've made the right choice, by the way. I know I'm biased because, well, I was born! So maybe, in a way, we can all be a little grateful to Stepan Dmitrievich. Or because it was the easier choice?"

"Your great-grandpa could have been arrested. Almost anyone could have been arrested," Masha says. "I didn't know it then."

She is already regretting having told the story to her great-granddaughter, who is smart but seems to lack a certain kind of imagination.

"I still don't understand how you could not have known anything. Did you feel like you were in a fairy tale, in a kind of horror fairy tale?"

For a moment Masha wants to slap the girl.

"You, a grown girl with such odd, public ambitions, you should clean the wax out of your ears, trim the claws of your heart. Pull back the curtains."

WINTER

The grackles flap dark & showy into my sleep.

I know they are only my synapses sparking pretty hallucinations but still they
flaunt their rough & many consonants.

Kellogg's! Lacuna! Grief counseling!

These are the sounds they like to make.

Then they ask about my mother & father, whether I've spoken to them lately.

In this way, they are just like my boyfriend.

I tell them my cell service is terrible, that I often think of switching, & then
the company texts me, *Thank you for being a valued member of our community!*

The grackles say to speak more slowly. They are still learning human.

It starts to snow & I wish I lived alone, in Paris.

Or maybe in my parents' house, without my parents.

My boyfriend's mother lives in a box.

My boyfriend lives with his mother in slow, not quite stories during breakfast.

I wish I wasn't tired of his sadness.

But I'd rather look at the snow, falling like silver confetti, another pretty
    thing my mind can make.

I wonder if I'd be a better person if I learned to speak bird.

The grackles say I should learn to pick up the phone.

I ask for a different assignment.

Call, the grackles say. *Call back.*

THE SCHOOL OF NIGHT & HYPHENS

The sky tonight, so without aliens. The woods, very lacking
in witches. But the people, as usual, replete

with people. & so you, with your headset, sit
in the home office across the hall, stuck in a hell

of strangers crying, computers dying, the new
father's dropped-in-toilet baby

photos, the old Canadian, her grandson Gregory,
all-grown-up-now Greg, who gave her this phone

but won't call her. You call her
wonderful. You encourage her to tell you what's wrong

with her device. You with your good-at-your-job
good-looking-ness, I bet even over the phone

it's visible. I bet all the Canadian grandmas
want you, but hey, you're with me. Hey, take off

that headset. Steal away from your post. Cross
the hall, you sings-the-chorus-too-soon, you

makes-a-killer-veggie-taco, you
played-tennis-in-college-build, you Jeffrey, you

Jeff-ship full of stars, cauldron full of you,
come teach me a little bit

of nothing, in the dark
abundant hours.

THE CARRYING

The sky's white with November's teeth,
and the air is ash and woodsmoke.
A flush of color from the dying tree,
a cargo train speeding through, and there,
that's me, standing in the wintering
grass watching the dog suffer the cold
leaves. I'm not large from this distance,
just a fence post, a hedge of holly.
Wider still, beyond the rumble of overpass,
mares look for what's left of green
in the pasture, a few weanlings kick
out, and theirs is the same sky, white
like a calm flag of surrender pulled taut.
A few farms over, there's our mare,
her belly barrel-round with foal, or idea
of foal. It's Kentucky, late fall, and any
mare worth her salt is carrying the next
potential stake's winner. Ours, her coat
thicker with the season's muck, leans against
the black fence and this image is heavy
within me. How my own body, empty,
clean of secrets, knows how to carry her,
knows we were all meant for something.

WOULD YOU RATHER

Remember that car ride to Sea-Tac, how your sister's kids
        played a frenzied game of *Would You Rather*, where each choice

ticktocked between superpowers and towering piles of a food too-often denied,
        Would You Rather

have fiery lasers that shoot out of your eyes or eat sundaes with whip cream for every meal?

We dealt it out quick,
        without stopping to check ourselves for the truth.

We played so hard that I got good at the questions, learned
        there had to be an equality

to each weighted ask. Now, I'm an expert at comparing things
that give the illusion they equal each other.

You said our Plan B was just to live our lives: more time, more sleep, travel—

        and still I'm making a list of all the places
I found out I wasn't carrying a child.

At the outdoor market in San Telmo, Isla Negra's wide iris of sea,
the baseball stadium, the supermarket, the Muhammad Ali museum, but always

the last time tops the list, in the middle of the Golden Gate Bridge,
looking over toward Alcatraz, a place they should burn and redeliver

to the gulls and cormorants, common daisies and sea grass.

Down below the girder that's still not screened against jumpers,
so that it seems almost like a dare, an invitation,

    we watched a seal make a sinuous shimmy in the bay.

Would you rather? Would I rather? The game is endless and without a winner.

Do you remember how the seal was so far under the deafening sound
of traffic, the whir of wind mixed with car horns and gasoline, such a small

speck of black movement alone in the churning waves
    between rock and shore?

Didn't she seem happy?

MAYBE I'LL BE ANOTHER KIND OF MOTHER

Snow today, a layer outlining the maple like a halo,
or rather, a fungus. So many sharp edges in the month.

I'm thinking I'll never sit down at the table
at the restaurant, you know that one, by the window?

Women gathered in paisley scarves with rusty iced tea,
talking about their kids, their little time-suckers,

how their mouths want so much, a gesture of exhaustion,
a roll of the eyes, *But I wouldn't have it any other way,*

their bags full of crayons and nut-free snacks, the light
coming in the window, a small tear of joy melting like ice.

No, I'll be elsewhere, having spent all day writing words
and then at the movies, where my man bought me a drink,

because our bodies are our own, and what will it be?
A blockbuster? A man somewhere saving the world, alone,

with only the thought of his family to get him through.
The film will be forgettable, a thin star in a blurred sea of stars,

I'll come home and rub my whole face against my dog's
belly; she'll be warm and want to sleep some more.

I'll stare at the tree and the ice will have melted, so
it's only the original tree again, green branches giving way

to other green branches, everything coming back to life.

She Was Warned

In a room for women whose bodies are broken, the biographer waits her turn. She wears sweat pants, is white skinned and freckle cheeked, not young, not old. Before she is called to climb into stirrups and feel her vagina prodded with a wand that makes black pictures, on a screen, of her ovaries and uterus, the biographer sees every wedding ring in the room. Serious rocks, fat bands of glitter. They live on the fingers of women who have leather sofas and solvent husbands but whose cells and tubes and bloods are failing at their animal destiny.

Leni Zumas

This, anyway, is the story the biographer likes. It is a simple, easy story that allows her not to think about what's happening in the women's heads, or in the heads of the husbands who sometimes accompany them.

Nurse Crabby wears a neon-pink wig and a plastic-strap contraption that exposes nearly all of her torso, including a good deal of breast. "Happy Halloween," she explains.

"And to you," says the biographer.

"Let's go suck out some lineage."

"Pardon?"

"Anagram for blood."

"Hmm," says the biographer politely.

Crabby doesn't find the vein straight off. Has to dig, and it hurts. "Where *are* you, mister?" she asks the vein. Months of needlework have streaked and darkened the insides of the biographer's elbows. Luckily long sleeves are common in this part of the world.

"Aunt Flo visited again, did she?" says Crabby.

"Vengefully."

"Well, Roberta, the body's a riddle. Here we go—*got* you." Blood swooshes into the chamber. It will tell them how much follicle-stimulating hormone and estradiol and progesterone the biographer's body is making. There are good numbers and there are bad. Crabby drops the tube into a rack alongside other little bullets of blood.

Half an hour later, a knock on the exam-room door—a warning, not a request for permission. In comes a man wearing leather trousers, aviator sunglasses, a curly black wig under a porkpie hat.

"I'm Slash," says Dr. Kalbfleisch.

"Wow," says the biographer, bothered by how sexy he's become.

"Shall we take a look?" He settles his leather on a stool in front of her open legs, says, "Oops!" and removes the sunglasses. Kalbfleisch played football at an East Coast university and still has the face of a frat boy. He is golden skinned, a poor listener. He smiles while citing bleak statistics. The nurse holds the biographer's file and a pen to write measurements. The doctor will call out how thick the lining, how large the follicles, how many the follicles. Add these numbers to the biographer's age (42) and her level

---

From the novel *Red Clocks*, forthcoming from Lee Boudreaux Books in January.

of follicle-stimulating hormone (14.3) and the temperature outside (56) and the number of ants in the square foot of soil directly beneath them (87), and you get the odds. The chance of a child.

Snapping on latex gloves: "Okay, Roberta, let's see what's what."

On a scale of one to ten, with ten being the shrill funk of aged cheese and one being no odor at all, how would he rank the smell of the biographer's vagina? How does it compare with the other vaginas barreling through this exam room, day in, day out, years of vaginas, a crowd of vulvic ghosts? Plenty of women don't shower beforehand, or are battling a yeast, or just happen naturally to stink in the nethers. Kalbfleisch has sniffed some ripe tangs in his time.

He slides in the ultrasound wand, dabbed with its blue jelly, and presses it up against her cervix. "Your lining's nice and thin," he says. "Four point five. Right where we want it." On the monitor, the lining of the biographer's uterus is a dash of white chalk in a black swell, hardly enough of a thing, it seems, to measure, but Kalbfleisch is a trained professional in whose expertise she is putting her trust. And her money—so much money that the numbers seem virtual, mythical, details from a story about money rather than money anyone actually has. The biographer, for example, does not have it. She's using credit cards.

> The doctor moves to the ovaries, shoving and tilting the wand until he gets an angle he likes.

The doctor moves to the ovaries, shoving and tilting the wand until he gets an angle he likes. "Here's the right side. Nice bunch of follicles . . ." The eggs themselves are too small to be seen, even with magnification, but their sacs—black holes on the grayish screen—can be counted.

"Keep our fingers crossed," says Kalbfleisch, easing the wand back out.

Doctor, is my bunch actually nice?

He rolls away from her crotch and pulls off his gloves. "For the past several cycles"—looking at her chart—"you've been taking Clomid to support ovulation."

This she does not need to be told.

"Unfortunately Clomid also causes the uterine lining to shrink, so we advise patients not to take it for long stretches of time. You've already done a long stretch."

Wait, what?

She should have looked it up herself.

"So for this round we need to try a different protocol. Another medication that's been known to improve the odds in some elderly pregravid cases."

"Elderly?"

"Merely a clinical term." He doesn't glance up from the prescription he's writing. "She'll explain the medication and we'll see you back here on day nine." He hands the file to the nurse, stands, and makes an adjustment to his leather crotch before striding out.

"So you need to fill this today," says Crabby, "and start taking it tomorrow morning, on an empty stomach. Every morning for ten days. While you're on it, you might notice a foul odor from the discharge from your vagina."

"Great," says the biographer.

"Some women say the smell is quite, um, surprising," she goes on. "Even actually disturbing. But whatever you do, don't douche. Questions?"

The water heaves up for reasons they don't have names for.

"What does"—the biographer squints at the prescription—"Ovutran do?"

"It supports ovulation."

"How, though?"

"You'd have to ask the doctor."

She is submitting her area to all kinds of invasion without understanding a fraction of what's being done to it. This seems, suddenly, terrible.

"I'd like to ask him now," she says.

"He's already with another patient. Best thing to do is call the office."

"But I'm here. In the office. Is there someone else who—"

"Sorry, it's an extra-busy day. Halloween and all."

"Why does Halloween make it busier?"

"It's a holiday."

"Not a *national* holiday. Banks are open and the mail is delivered."

"You will need," says Crabby slowly, carefully, "to call the office."

The biographer cried the first time it failed. She was waiting in line to buy floss, having pledged to improve her dental hygiene now that she was going to be a parent, and her phone rang: one of the nurses, "I'm sorry, sweetie, but your test was negative," the biographer saying thank you, okay, thank you and hitting END before the tears started. Despite the statistics and Kalbfleisch's "This doesn't work for everyone," the biographer had thought it would be easy. Squirt in millions of sperm from a nineteen-year-old biology major, precisely timed to be there waiting when the egg flies out; sperm and egg collide in the warm tunnel—how could fertilization *not* happen?

Don't be stupid anymore, she wrote in her notebook, under *Immediate action required*.

She drives west on Highway 22 into dark hills dense with hemlock, fir, and spruce. Oregon has the best trees in America, soaring and shaggy winged, alpine sinister. Her tree gratitude mutes her doctor resentment. Two hours from his office, her car crests the cliff road and the church steeple juts into view. The rest of town follows, hunched in rucked hills sloping to the water. Smoke coils from the pub chimney. Fishing nets pile on the shore. In Newville you can watch the sea eat the ground, over and over, unstopping. Millions of abyssal thalassic acres. The sea does not ask permission or wait for instruction. It doesn't suffer from not knowing what on earth, exactly, it is meant to do. Today its walls are high, white lather torn. "Angry sea," people say, but to the biographer the ascribing of human feeling to a body so inhumanly itself is wrong. The water heaves up for reasons they don't have names for.

For seven years she has lived in the lee of fog-smoked evergreen mountains, thousand-foot cliffs plunging straight down to the Pacific. It rains and rains and rains. Log trucks stall traffic on the cliff road, the pub hangs a list of old shipwrecks, the tsunami siren is tested monthly, and students learn to say "miss" as if they were servants.

The pharmacist's assistant is a boy—now a young man—she taught in her first year at Central Coast Regional High School, and she hates the moment each month when he hands her the white bag with the little orange bottle. *I know what this is for*, his eyes say. Even if his eyes don't actually say that, it's hard to look at him. She brings other items to the counter (unsalted peanuts, Q-tips) as if somehow to disguise the fertility medication. The biographer can't recall his name but remembers admiring, in class, seven years ago, his long black lashes—they always looked a little wet.

Waiting on the hard plastic chair, under elevator music and fluorescent glare, the biographer takes out her notebook. Everything in this notebook must be in list form, and any list is eligible. *Items for next food shop. Kalbfleisch's necktie designs. Countries with most lighthouses per capita.*

She starts a new one: *Accusations from the world.*

1. You're too old.
2. If you can't have a child the natural way, you shouldn't have one at all.
3. Every child needs two parents.
4. Children raised by single mothers are more liable to rape/ murder/drug-take/score low on standardized tests.
5. You're too old.
6. You should've thought of this earlier.
7. You're selfish.
8. You're doing something unnatural.
9. How is that child going to feel when she finds out her father is an anonymous masturbator?
10. Your body is a grizzled husk.
11. You're too old, sad spinster!
12. Are you only doing this because you're lonely?

"Miss? Prescription's ready."

"Thank you." She signs the screen on the counter. "How's your day going?"

Lashes turns up his palms at the ceiling.

"If it makes you feel any better," says the biographer, "my new medication is going to make me have a foul-smelling vaginal discharge."

"At least it's for a good cause."

She clears her throat.

"That'll be one hundred fifty-seven dollars and sixty-three cents," he adds.

"Pardon me?"

"I'm really sorry."

"A hundred and fifty-seven dollars? For ten pills?"

"Your insurance doesn't cover it."

"Why the eff not?"

Lashes shakes his head. "I wish I could, like, slip it to you, but they've got cameras on every inch of this bitch."

She can't see the ocean from her apartment, but she can hear it. Most days between 5:00 and 6:30 AM she sits in the kitchen listening to the waves and working on her study of Eivør Mínervudottír, a nineteenth-century hydrologist from the Faroe Islands whose trailblazing research on pack ice was published under a male acquaintance's name. There is no book on Mínervudottír, only passing mentions in other books. The biographer has a mass of notes by now, an outline, some paragraphs. A skein draft—more holes than words. On the kitchen wall she's taped a photo of the shelf in the Salem bookstore where her book might someday reside.

She opens Mínervudottír's journal, translated from the Danish. *I admit to fearing the attack of a sea bear; and my fingers hurt all the time.* A woman long dead coming to life. But today, staring at the journal, the biographer can't think. Her brain is soapy and throbbing from the new medication.

Two years ago the US Congress ratified the Personhood Amendment, which gives the constitutional right to life, liberty, and property to a fertilized egg at the moment of conception. Abortion is now illegal in all fifty states. Abortion providers can be charged with second-degree murder, abortion seekers with conspiracy to commit murder. In vitro fertilization, too, is federally banned, because the amendment outlaws the transfer of embryos from laboratory to uterus. (The embryos can't give their consent to be moved.)

She was warned, yes, at the outset: birth mothers tend to choose married straight couples.

She was just quietly teaching history when it happened. Woke up one morning to a president-elect she hadn't voted for. This man thought women who miscarried should pay for funerals for the fetal tissue and thought a lab technician who accidentally dropped an embryo during in vitro transfer was guilty of manslaughter. After his victory there was glee on the lawns of her father's Orlando retirement village. Marching in the streets of Portland. In Newville: brackish calm.

Short of sex with some man she wouldn't otherwise want to have sex with, Ovutran and lube-glopped vaginal wands and Dr. Kalbfleisch's golden fingers is the only biological route left. Intrauterine insemination. At her age, not much better than a turkey baster.

She was placed on the adoption waiting list three years ago. In her parent profile she earnestly and meticulously described her job, her apartment, her favorite books, her parents, her brother (drug addiction omitted), and the fierce beauty of Newville. She uploaded a photograph that made her look friendly but responsible, fun loving but stable, easygoing but middle class. The coral-pink cardigan she bought to wear in this photo she later threw into the clothing donation bin outside the church.

She was warned, yes, at the outset: birth mothers tend to choose married straight couples, especially if the couple is white. But not all birth mothers choose this way. Anything could happen, she was told. The fact that she was willing to take an older child or a child who needed special care meant the odds were in her favor.

She assumed it would take a while but that it would, eventually, happen.

She thought a foster placement, at least, would come through; and if things went well, that could lead to adoption.

Then the new president moved into the White House.

The Personhood Amendment was passed.

One of the ripples in its wake: Public Law 116-72.

> Her okayness with being by herself—ordinary, unheroic okayness—does not need to justify itself to her father.

On January 15—in less than three months—this law, also known as Every Child Needs Two, will take effect. Its mission: *to restore dignity, strength, and prosperity to American families.* Unmarried persons will be legally prohibited from adopting children. In addition to valid marriage licenses, all adoptions will require approval through a federally regulated agency, rendering private transactions criminal.

Her father is calling again. It has been days—weeks?—since she answered.

"How's Florida?"

"I am curious to know your plans for Christmas."

"Two months away, Dad."

"But you'll want to book the flight soon. Fares are going to explode. When does school let out?"

"I don't know, the twenty-third?"

"That close to Christmas? Jesus."

"I'll let you know, okay?"

"Any plans for the weekend?"

"Friends invited me to dinner. You?"

"Might drop by the community center to watch the human rutabagas gum their feed. Unless my back flares up."

"What did the acupuncturist say?"

"*That* was a mistake I won't make twice."

"It works for a lot of people, Dad."

"It's goddamn voodoo. Will you be bringing a date to your friends' dinner?"

"Nope," says the biographer, steeling herself for his next sentence, her face stiff with sadness that he can't help himself.

"About time you found someone, don't you think?"

"I'm fine."

"Well, I *worry*, kiddo. Don't like the idea of you being all alone."

She could trot out the usual list ("I've got friends, neighbors, coworkers, people from meditation group"), but her okayness with being by herself—ordinary, unheroic okayness—does not need to justify itself to her father. The feeling is hers. She can simply feel okay and not explain it, or apologize for it, or concoct arguments against the argument that she doesn't *truly* feel content and is deluding herself in self-protection.

"Well, Dad," she says, "you're alone too."

Any reference to her mother's death can be relied on to shut him up.

Before the first insemination, the biographer forced herself to consult online dating sites. She browsed and bared her teeth. She browsed and felt chest-flatteningly depressed. One night she really did try. Picked the least Christian site and started typing.

What are your three best qualities?

1. Independence
2. Punctuality
3.

Best book you recently read?
Ice Ghosts: The Epic Hunt for the Lost Franklin Expedition

What fascinates you?

1. How cold stops water
2. Patterns ice makes on the fur of a dead sled dog
3. The fact that Eivør Mínervudottír lost two of her fingers to frostbite

But the biographer didn't feel like telling anyone those things. Delete, delete, delete. She could say, at least, she had tried. The next day she called for an appointment at a reproductive-medicine clinic in Salem.

Her therapist thought she was moving fast. "You only recently decided to do this," he said, "and already you've chosen a donor?"

Oh, therapist, if only you knew how quickly a donor can be chosen! You turn on your computer. You click boxes for race, eye color, education, height. A list appears. You read some profiles. You hit PURCHASE.

A woman on the Choosing Single Motherhood discussion board wrote: *I spent more time deadheading my roses than picking a donor.*

But, as the biographer explained to her therapist, she did *not* choose quickly. She pored. She strained. She sat for hours at her kitchen table, staring at profiles. These men had written essays. Named personal strengths. Recalled moments of childhood jubilance and described favorite traits of grandparents. (For one hundred dollars per ejaculation, they were happy to discuss their grandparents.)

"Do you feel undeserving of a romantic partner?" asked the therapist.

"No," said the biographer.

"Are you pessimistic about finding a partner?"

"I don't *want* a partner."

"Might that attitude be a form of self-protection?"

"You mean am I deluding myself?"

"That's another way to put it."

"If I say yes, then I'm not deluded. And if I say no, it's further evidence of delusion."

"We need to end there," said the therapist.

The dawn air is cold and gritty with salt. She sits in her car, throat shivering with hints of vomit, until she's late enough not to care that her eye–foot–brake reaction time is slowed by the Ovutran. The roads have guardrails. Her forehead pulses hard. She sees a black lace throw itself across the windshield, and blinks it away.

She can't face the drive to her day-nine egg-check appointment without coffee, even though caffeine is on Hawthorne Reproductive Medicine's list of things to avoid. Teeth on her mug, she steers up the hill, under towering balsam fir and Sitka spruce, away her town. Newville gets ninety-eight inches of rain a year. The inland fields are quaggy, hard to farm. Cliff roads slick in winter. Storms so bad they sink boats and tear roofs from houses. The biographer likes these problems because they keep people away—the people who might otherwise move here, that is, not the tourists, who cruise in on dry summer asphalt and don't give a sea onion about farming.

Kalbfleisch calls her ultrasound "encouraging." The biographer has five follicles measuring twelve and thirteen, plus a gaggle of smallers. "You'll be ready for insemination right on schedule, I suspect. Day fourteen. Which is . . ." He leans back, waits for the nurse to open the calendar and count off the squares with her finger. "Wednesday. Do we have at least a couple of vials here?" As usual, he doesn't look at her, even when asking a direct question.

Four, in fact, are sitting in the clinic's frozen storage, tiny bottles of ejaculate from the scrota of a college sophomore majoring in biology (3811) and a rock-climbing enthusiast who described his sister as "extremely beautiful" (9072). She also owns some semen from 5546, a personal trainer who baked a cake for sperm-bank staff; but his remaining vials are still at the bank in Los Angeles.

"Start the OPKs tomorrow or the next day," says Kalbfleisch. "Fingers crossed." He rubs foaming sanitizer into his palms.

"By the way." She sits up on the exam table, covers her crotch with the paper sheet. "Is it possible I've got polycystic ovary syndrome?"

> Her forehead pulses hard. She sees a black lace throw itself across the windshield, and blinks it away.

Kalbfleisch stops midrub. A golden frown. "Why do you ask?"

"I don't have *all* the symptoms, but—"

"Roberta, were you looking online?" He sighs. "You can diagnose yourself with anything and everything online. First of all, the majority of women with PCOS are overweight, and you are not."

"Okay, so you don't—"

"Although." He is looking at her, but not in the eye. More in the mouth. "You do have excessive facial hair. And, come to think of it, excessive body hair. Which is a symptom."

Come to think of it? "But, um, how does that account for genetics? Certain ethnic groups are naturally hairier. My mom's grandmothers both had mustaches."

"I can't speak to that," says Kalbfleisch. "I'm not an anthropologist. I do know that hirsutism is a sign of PCOS."

Wouldn't that be human biology, in which all physicians are trained, and not anthropology?

"When you come in on—" He glances at the nurse.

"Wednesday," she says.

"—I'll take a closer look at your ovaries, and we'll include a testosterone check with your bloodwork."

"If I have PCOS, what does that mean?"

"That the odds of your conceiving via intrauterine insemination are exceedingly low."

She wants an ashy line down the center of a round belly. She wants nausea. The marks of motherhood on her friend Susan: spider veins at the knee backs, loose stomach skin, lowered breasts. Affronts to vanity worn as badges of the ultimate accomplishment.

But why does she want them, really? Because Susan has them? Because the Salem bookstore manager has them? Because she always vaguely assumed she would have them herself? Or does the desire come from some creaturely place, precivilized, some biological throb that floods her blood-ways with the message *Make more of yourself!* To repeat, not to improve. It doesn't matter to the ancient throb if she does good works in this short life—if she publishes, for instance, a magnificent book on Eivør Miner-vudottír that would give people pleasure and knowledge. The throb simply wants another human machine that can, in turn, make another.

How can you raise a child alone when you can't resist twelve ounces of coffee?

When you've been known to eat peanut butter on a spoon for dinner?

When you often go to bed without brushing your teeth?

Ab ovo. The twin eggs of Leda, impregnated by Zeus in swan form: one hatched into Helen, who would launch ships. Start from the beginning. Except there is no beginning. Can the biographer remember first thinking, feeling, or deciding she wanted to be someone's mother? The original moment of longing to let a bulb of lichen grow in her until it came out human? The longing is widely endorsed. Legislators, aunts, and advertisers approve. Which makes the longing, she thinks, a little suspicious.

Babies once were abstractions. They were *Maybe I do, but not now.* The biographer used to sneer at talk of biological deadlines, believing the topic to be crap for lifestyle magazines. Women who worried about ticking clocks were the same women who traded salmon-loaf recipes and asked their husbands to clean the gutters. She was not and never would be one of them.

Then, suddenly, she was one of them. Not the gutters, but the clock. ◈

INSTRUCTIONS PRIOR

The tickseed thriving in banks like clouds beneath us

The idea of a wind

The clean commitment every instinct comes down to in the hawk descending

Actual wind, waves as waves

The idea of a body

Waves as merely interruptions for once across the lake's flat surface

Only what you yourself mean to it, yes

Your idea of the world

The body as a shield keeping slightly at bay what it also reflects

Everything you've lived for

Its raised wings machete-ing the space between want and having

For hours, I lay beside him in the pear tree's shadow, watching him sleep.

IS IT TRUE ALL LEGENDS ONCE WERE RUMORS

And it was as we'd been told it would be: some stumbling wingless;
others flew beheaded. But at first when we looked at them, we could
see no difference, the way it can take a while to realize about how
regretfulness is not regret. As for being frightened: though for many
animals the governing instinct, when most afraid, is to attack, what about
the tendency of songbirds, in a storm, toward silence—is that fear, too?
For mostly, yes, we were silent—tired, as well, though as much out of
boredom as for the need to stretch a bit, why not the rest on foot, we
at last decided—and dismounting, each walked with his horse close
beside him. We mapped our way north by the stars, old school, until there
were no stars, just the weather of childhood, where it's snowing forever.

MOON AND STAR

Ginger Gaffney

Horses and Inmates Share the Pen

Luna's wound site is swollen and full of pus. Her right eye shut, padded like an overstuffed pillow ready to blow. There's a trickle of yellow ooze squeezing out from its corner, where the infection has sunk beneath the surface of a five-inch zigzag crack that blazes across the center of her face. Without some attention, and a long round of antibiotics, Luna will lose that eye.

Aside from her swollen face, Luna is on her A game. She and her sister Estrella, both black-and-white paint horses, each with one blue eye, have roamed free on this seventeen-acre ranch. The two mares have been uncatchable for the last two years. The ranch's residents have chased them into every corner, every structure, even into this seventy-foot round pen. No one's been able to lay a hand on them. One of the residents, a part-time team roper, part-time drug smuggler from Las Cruces, ran Luna into a stall one afternoon three weeks ago and tried to rope her. His loop fell halfway across her face as she reared up and smacked her head on the twelve-inch overhanging shelter beam. Blood splattered everywhere as Luna ran out of the shelter, knocking the cowboy off his feet

and catching her left hip on a T-post. Her flank sliced open like two pink lips parting.

Dr. Roger's been out two different times attempting to treat her. No luck. On his last visit, he left Sarah and Angie, the two women newly in charge of the horses at this prison-alternative ranch, my phone number, written with a black Sharpie on a yellow Post-it note and stapled to the tack room door. Angie's a heroin addict and a thief. She's on this ranch for two more years to fulfill her prison sentence. Sarah's a meth dealer and prostitute. She has four more years before she can begin to think outside these walls. Ever since Luna's accident, they have been made the leaders of the Livestock team, a crew of six men who are also filling their prison terms. Their first job in this new role is to get Luna the care she needs. Neither has any experience working with horses. They volunteered for the position anyway, knowing that Luna was in real trouble. They will help me separate the sisters, split their familial bond for the first time in two years.

Today, Luna and Estrella are hungry. We have skipped two days of feed to bait them into the round pen where we will lock the gate and try to catch them. Sarah shakes a bucket of grain at the mares, tempting them out from the alleyway behind the tall building where they seem to find security.

> Angie's a heroin addict and a thief. She's on this ranch for two more years to fulfill her prison sentence.

She walks across desert weeds and dry sagebrush dropping small piles of grain, hoping to lure the sisters across the field and over toward the round pen. The hot New Mexico summer sun is already high in the sky and it's only midmorning.

Estrella moves out in front of Luna and gobbles up the piles. Pieces of rolled oats fall from her mouth as she chews sideways and carelessly. Luna shoves her head to the ground to eat what Estrella has left behind. Pile by pile they walk slow and steady across the pasture toward the pen. Until now, Angie and I have stayed hidden inside the hay barn. As they get close, Angie heads out to the pen with two fat flakes of alfalfa. Luna and Estrella pick their heads up and watch when Angie opens the gate and places the flakes against the farthest wall. She turns and hurries back into the barn. Sarah advances. Her piles are now farther apart. She takes what's left of the grain and pours it out in the center of the pen. She climbs over the top rail and joins Angie and me in the hay barn.

Estrella comes through the gate first, like a wild cat slowly lifting each foot from the knee. She holds her leg up with just enough pause that it looks as though she's ready to pounce on a kill. Muzzle to the ground, her back arching high, her hindquarters dig in and sink under her body. She drops her head into the pile of grain. Sarah, Angie, and I watch from inside the barn, about one hundred feet from the pen. Luna enters aslant. She twists and turns in all directions, certain that trouble follows her everywhere. She bends over the tiny, bright green leaves of the alfalfa with a wary backward twitch of her ears. Sarah walks out from the barn with long, quiet steps and snaps the pen's gate closed behind them.

We move in closer and watch the sisters silently pick at the clover-sized leaves. The far reaches of their upper lips act like fingertips, dragging the miniature foliage onto their tongues. Luna's body trembles as she eats. We can see the shake of it across her topline where her long winter hairs bristle and shimmy across her spine. Estrella lets out a wet blow from her muzzle and continues chewing on the alfalfa. She's smaller and less athletic. With a short back and barreled belly, she almost looks pregnant. The hollowed-out dish in her nose tells me she is at least part Arab.

Sarah and Angie talk in whispers, hashing out some drama that happened in the women's dorm last night. Angie looks down at her hands and spreads each finger out wide, admiring her multicolored fingernails. They match the red and purple ribbons woven into her long black pony braid. There are already chips in two of her nails and we haven't even started yet. They huddle over this major disappointment until I break their reverie and remind them exactly why we're here today.

Angie's not even five-feet tall and Sarah has a wayward leg that curls out to the side of her body like a pirate's hook. With each stride the right side of her body collapses. I worry over how to keep them safe. We must enter this round pen like wolves: intimidating, fierce, respectable. Sarah is chewing on her cuticles as if they are question marks and Angie twists the end of her braid over and over.

"Angie, you ready?" I ask.

"Absolutely."

"You sure?"

Angie explained in our first meeting that she's a compulsive liar. She can't tell the truth from a lie. She's been that way most of her life. Around this ranch, she said, they call it false pride. But for Angie, it's more than that. She has a thin hold on what's real and what's not. Her many years of heroin addiction make knowing the difference difficult.

I pause and she recognizes that I'm waiting for her to pay better attention, to forget about her ponytail, her fingernails, and return to the business at hand.

"I'm not sure if I'm ready, Ms. Ginger. What do you want us to do?"

"I need you both to bend your knees, spread your arms and legs out wide, make yourselves bigger. Watch me." I bend down into an old basketball position, spread my

Now, directly in front of her, I howl an angry call, jump up and down and try my best to fill up with fury.

skinny frame out as far as it will go and start to slide sideways, right to left, then left to right, with my arms stretched and flapping like flags. "We have to make a wall, a straight line across that pen which will keep the sisters separate. We'll have to work as a team in there, one unit, no holes. If they see any space between us they're gonna try to break through."

To my right, Sarah crouches and starts to slide with me. Angie slides on my left. With our outstretched arms and legs, we create an entwined human wall. Straight and woven but still not strong enough to separate these mares.

"We need to practice. Angie, stand over there next to the cottonwood tree, please. Sarah, you can stay near the round pen. Bend your knees again and take your positions. And no matter what crazy shit I do, don't back away."

They laugh but know I'm not joking. Angie shifts her stance wide but gets distracted by a loose shoestring. Sarah can't stop sucking and picking at her fingers. Neither of them knows what's coming nor what to expect next. They listen, then they refocus. Angie bobs up and down on the toes of her sneakers, trying to prepare herself. Sarah sighs then bunches her fingers into fists. She bends slightly from her waist and brings her fists close to her chin like a boxer. All they want is to get Luna the help she needs.

I run down the road about a hundred feet from them and ask again if they're ready. They give me half nods and I haul up the road right at Angie. Screaming, growling, pinning my upper lip to the bottom of my nostrils. Angie sits low in her stance with her arms out in front, elbows bent, primed to defend herself if needed. As I get close, she breaks toward me and yips a cold sound that cracks from the narrow part of her throat. Her spit hits my face like a switch. Now, directly in front of her, I howl an angry call, jump up and down and try my best to fill up with fury. Angie returns a pitchy scream that sends pins and needles into my ears, followed by two big stomps close to my toes. I smell her guts, her reckless anchor. Sarah turns her head away and covers her face with her hands. Our staged version of a cockfight has her back tracking. Angie's arms swing wild, elbows knocking at mine. Luna and Estrella have stopped eating and have run to the far side of the pen. I look over at Sarah, who's beading up a sweat.

"Please don't do that to me," she says.

I drop my arms to my waist and turn to address Sarah.

She removes her hands from her face and says, "Maybe, maybe I'm not the right person for today."

"You are. You certainly are, just stick close to me." I wave them both together and bring them in front of me. "We're ready."

I watch as Angie and Sarah walk ahead of me toward the round pen. They look like a moving puzzle, broken pieces stuck momentarily together. I wonder how long we can hold our wall intact. Estrella's and Luna's ears follow us as we get closer. They run around the pen at a slow trot. The curves of their bodies move like schools of fish, neat and tucked, swinging in unison with each stride. I hear the crunch of gravel under my feet. I try to relax my shoulders. We must be whole for this to work. The horses will see us for who we are. We'll have no secrets, no lies to protect us. Just the honesty of our bodies.

We enter the round pen and latch the gate behind us. The two mares fly around the perimeter in a panic. Luna is out in front with Estrella close behind. Angie and Sarah are positioned off the wings of my shoulders, arms and legs spread wide, forming the needle of a rotating dial, a solid line across the center of the pen. Sarah and I walk forward as Angie moves backward, turning our needle counter-clockwise. When the mares up their pace, our walking turns into a run.

We're looking for a large enough gap between the sister bodies to step in and slice the two apart, put our woman-made wall in between them and break their bond. Angie sees an opening and slides sideways into the break, turning Estrella back to the right while Luna keeps spinning left. The separation cuts our pen and the sisters into two. All hell breaks loose.

Estrella turns back and forth. She tries to return to Luna, who screeches a piercing note that bounces off the adobe walls fortifying the borders of this ranch. Our needle spins as fast as Estrella. The two sisters peel around their separate hemispheres in a frenzy. The small pen makes our frames look larger than we are. Every turn Estrella

makes sends the needle turning in the opposite direction.

Behind us, Luna's in a tantrum. From the corner of my eye I catch glimpses of her stomping her front hooves to the ground, then rearing toward the sky, thrashing out with her front legs. Angie holds hard to her position, running forward then backward at Estrella's every turn. Her breath speaks in grunts. The dial spins round and round as our bodies struggle to keep our human wall in place. Sarah is tiring, her arms and legs shrinking closer to her body as her energy wanes. She's crossing her legs behind instead of sliding, tripping herself up on each rotation.

Estrella swoops back to the right and our needle whirls around with her. Sarah loses her balance and goes down on one knee. Estrella finds the hole. She breaks through the rift in our wall and gallops back to Luna, catching Sarah's crooked leg and knocking her, face first, to the ground. Luna's screaming halts. The mares meet up and flank each other, two bodies become one.

Luna's roars have pulled in a crowd. Residents gather from all around the ranch. I see the men from Livestock arrive. They lean heavy on the upper rail of the pen. Their curiosity and questions cause a deep distraction for Angie and Sarah. Sarah picks herself up and slaps at the dust covering her right side. Her face is covered in a pink shade of brown and her forehead is scraped and pocked with small pebbles. A contagion of adrenaline starts to swirl around us. A mindless fever. A thousand black starlings cackling into the sky.

"Quiet, quiet!" I call out. "You are welcome to stay, but please be quiet. And step back, please, two feet from the rail."

I set the boundaries and everyone comes to a hush while Angie, Sarah, and I return to our positions. I can see doubt forming on their faces. Like maybe we won't be able to do this. Won't be able to catch them or halter them. We won't be able to separate them and get Luna the help she needs. Sarah looks at the ground and kicks at the dirt. Angie hasn't spoken a word since the crowd gathered.

"You guys alright?" I walk over to Sarah, put my hand on her shoulder and check the gashes in her forehead. "We can stop if you need to," I say, "and start again tomorrow." Angie walks over and stands so close I feel the heat of her body on my face.

"I'm not stopping. No way. Look at her." She juts her chin at Luna. "We've gotta help her, *today*." We turn toward Luna and see the yellow pus drooling across her cheek. Angie's arms are relaxed and down by her sides. Her breath is even and she holds her head at such a tilt I can see her nostrils flaring in and out. She's calm, she's confident, and she's ready.

Sarah agrees. We get back into our positions, which sends the sisters rushing around the perimeter of the pen. Luna leads once again. Estrella dragging behind now. She's tiring. Her footfall is no longer fueled by panic and fear. Angie steps into the slot and the connection between Estrella and Luna is broken again.

Sliding together, long strokes, we move as a band of feral horses, no gaps. We displace Luna's torment into the back of our minds as Estrella starts to make a change. She's running half-rounds now, pivoting off our cue as we swing our needle left to right, right to left in a syncopated dance. A quiet balance comes over her. She runs for five more minutes and stops, parallel with the rail, breathing heavy, her blue eye facing us. I see something familiar in her. A welcomed acceptance, her wildness disrobed, her domestic breeding peeking through.

Luna's roars have pulled in a crowd. Residents gather from all around the ranch.

We stay motionless and let Estrella rest. Her body quivers, muscles loosen their grip. Her mind begins to untie itself from Luna. I move toward her from the center of the ring. If she is to take a step or try to bolt, Angie and Sarah have my corners and can cut her back. I reach out to touch her, scratch her neck and shoulders, the middle of her chest. She sucks in a half-caught gulp of air and then blows out the extra with one soft snort.

Angie and Sarah are torn up. Tears catch on their lower lashes. Getting close to either Luna or Estrella has been a dream over these last two years. This ranch is small. Every person, every animal is tied to the whole. Luna and Estrella have been on their own, isolated and traumatized, for far too long. I get the feeling Angie and Sarah know what it's like to live that way.

We keep an eye out for Luna, who's pacing back and forth in the other half of the pen, pitching a mournful wail every few strides. I leave Estrella and hustle to the box that holds the purple and red halters Angie has picked out for today, the same colors as her fingernails. I take soft steps back to Estrella and resume my hand massage with the halter and lead line draped over my shoulder.

We all come from somewhere, but that does not mean we belong.

Without even the slightest flinch, Estrella lets me slide the noseband over her muzzle. I latch the brass buckle, and Estrella follows behind as I move toward the gate. I know now that Estrella has been handled by humans before she came to this ranch. She accepts my touch, offers a quick sense of trust. Horses who are damaged don't make these changes with ease. Luna has stopped her desperate calls and for the first time stands quiet, watching Estrella walk away. Everything is crisp, clean, silent. I gesture for Angie to come get Estrella. We change places.

At a slow walk, Sarah, Angie, and Estrella exit the pen. Estrella's head and neck are low and swing loose from her body. Her eyes are round glassy marbles. They no longer glance sideways looking for trouble. I'm amazed how fast she can

change families. It carves a piece of loneliness from the middle of my chest. As they stride out together, I notice Sarah's limp is gone. Her bent leg is straight as a walking cane.

I turn and widen my stance, waiting for Luna to burst toward her sister as she leaves the pen, but Luna is motionless, standing parallel to the rail on the opposite side. Her one good eye, a shotgun.

Angie told me how the sisters arrived at the ranch two years ago. They were dropped here by a small-time breeder from a nearby town.

"They're too small," he told the Livestock crew. But what he meant was, they're female. People like geldings. Neutered males bring a higher price and sell easy.

No one from Livestock knew enough to look in the trailer, to see if the horses had halters on, to ask the man if they'd been handled before. They swung open the trailer door while the owner banged on the side walls with a stick, trying to frighten the horses out. Luna and Estrella twisted and crashed against each other and then, in a panic, leaped out the back and took off across the pasture.

Angie asked the breeder if they had names.

"They ain't got none. They're sisters," he said. He slammed the trailer door and jogged around to the front cab of his truck, wishing them luck as he hurried out the gate, the Livestock team in his rearview mirror.

"Flunkies," Sarah said. "They're flunkies, just like us."

Barely touched. Thinly loved. Not even given a name.

We all come from somewhere, but that does not mean we belong. Sarah's mom tried to strangle her two weeks before she took her own life. Now, Sarah stands with her short beefy arms wrapped around Estrella's black-and-white neck, her head pressed into Estrella's forehead. Both close their eyes. Angie pulls down with her fingers and struggles to unravel the tangled knots locked solid into Estrella's mane. Inside my truck, I drink a cold bottle of water, catch my breath, and watch the three of them. About a half-dozen men gather around and dote over Estrella. On the back seat of my truck sits the lariat I brought over, hoping I would not need to use it. Resting flat and docile against the fabric, it looks nothing like the noose I may have to float over Luna's neck if I can't catch her.

Luna's no longer crying for her sister, no longer looking up. Her one open eyelid is half shut over her good eye. She paces around the perimeter, hits the middle of the gate, paces back again. A sick empty rhythm comes from her hooves. When horses are in distress, they turn inward and ignore the world around them. They look more like robots than animals of prey. No longer alert, their ears fall sideways and face the ground. They move like caged animals, purposeless.

They stand still, staring out into the distance, without even a blink.

I take another sip of water. My throat begins to burn. I know this sunken place. For the first six years of my life, I did not speak a word. Silence was my inheritance, like my blond hair and broad forehead. Like the worried wrinkles around my eyes. I came into this world a mute. I would not speak, not even in the confines of my own room. I lived in a dead space, where silence kept me protected. Language was not to me what it is to most people: power. It was more like a knife, cutting everything apart. I hid. I ran from language. I fell asleep without dreams.

Luna's head has sunk low to the ground. She has quit her pacing and stands shoved up against the corral wall. I lean back, pick up the lariat from the seat of my truck, and walk over to the round pen.

The men from Livestock move away from Estrella and place themselves around the outside of the pen, like boulders, just as I begin to make my underhand loop. Pain enters my body through my eyes. I see in Luna's lifeless body what I must do. Get her the care, the help she needs. She looks half dead before I start to swing, but then she wakes and takes off to a gallop. I'm not surprised. I looked half dead myself once.

Luna's not interested in what I have to offer. She has that break in her, either she was born with it, or someone put it in her. Either way, she has no home. I'll have to make her come to us. Not ask her, not love her, nor try to change her. I'll have to rope her.

Angles. It's all about angles. Three, four, five feet. I've got to think ahead. Step back behind her. Straight across from her and all I'll do is throw this loop right at the side of her face. This loop must come in like an unseen cloud, something that drops in and over her before she knows what has happened. If I miss, if I hit her face with this rawhide hanger, she'll try to break through and over these walls.

Some of the men have their hands on their hips, legs spread past the width of their bodies, as Luna peels around the pen. Others hold their arms out wide, waving them, trying to distract her. She races around the pen in a rage, watching my loop grow. Sweat drips down the back of her legs, her ears are flat, and her tail is pinched up between her butt cheeks. She's ready to kick the shit out of me if I get too close.

As I count, my loop grows slowly. It's long and narrow and I need it wider. I flatten my elbow, move it close to my body, and straighten my wrist. My hand faces the sky as my loop bloats big enough to cover half her body. One . . . two . . . three, I let it fly. It's coming up from behind her, shoots out in front like a massive Frisbee, and hovers. It's three feet ahead of her when she freaks, kicks herself into fifth gear to outrun it, and the loop drops in around her shoulders.

Take out the slack. I think. *Damn it take out the slack. Don't let it slide down toward her legs and tangle things up.* I'm running backward. Coiling my lariat, snatching it up around her neck. I grab the rope with both hands and tuck my arms close to my body, ready for her to hit the end. Contact. She's in the

air. Her front legs jump above my line, she turns and the lariat pulls from under her belly. She's tangled and pissed. She's thrashing her front legs at the line as she gallops around trying to unravel herself. One more turn around the pen, hopping and bucking, and the rope hangs again from her neck. I coil the lariat tighter, grab hold, and with all 122 pounds of me, I pull her around and she faces me at a halt. Steaming.

She bolts. Again she turns, trying to outrun the connection but there's nowhere to go. We're tied to each other. Fifteen more minutes of wheeling, back and forth. I'm coiling the lariat in, closer and closer. I have her five feet in front of me at a standstill. I can smell the stench of her infected face from here. I'm not making a friend today. Today, I'm gonna save that eye.

I move off to the side of her, not too close to her hindquarters, and fold her neck around to her rib cage. From this position she'll have to bend those hindquarters under her body and re-face me. From this position, she can't bolt and she can't level me. I bend her side to side, for ten more minutes, until her neck feels half as stiff. My mouth is dry, my jaw tight, my skin trembles with a cold sweat tingling under my shirt.

"Two men. Two men," I shake the words from the back of my throat. "I need two volunteers. Somebody get the hose hooked up to the hydrant. We need to clean her up."

Tony jumps the round pen wall.

"I can hold her," he says. I have Luna's head bent so close to her body her muscles are shaking. The lariat burns in my hands.

"You can't let her straighten out. You can't trust her," I tell Tony. "She'll line her hindquarters up and kick the hell out of you."

"I got the hose!" Rex yells then pulls the green snaking monster toward Luna. She gurgles and huffs at it like it's going to kill her.

"Slow! Go slow, Rex!" I shout at him, then pump my palms to the ground to settle him down. "Turn up the water. Just a little at a time, please. We don't need to spook her any more than she is."

I hear the squeaky hydrant handle lift upward and a dribble of water slips from the mouth of the hose.

"Ready, Tony?" I ask.

He nods one quick bump of his head, Rex holds up the end of the hose, and the water starts to leak across Luna's face. She twists her head in jerks trying to get loose, opening her mouth then snapping her teeth together. *Clack. Clack. Clack.* She's fighting for her life.

"It's only water, Luna," I say in a soft voice, then tell Paul, who's over at the hydrant, to pull the handle up a little farther. Water is pouring over Luna's face. Tony has her in a firm grip. Luna's good eye twitches back and forth looking for what might come next.

"Turn the water off," I say to Paul. The hose runs dry. "Tony, with your right hand, can you scratch her a little?" I know if we take this in stages, Luna will learn to trust us.

Tony takes the edge of his fingernails and scratches the bumpy mosquito bites that cover her neck.

"More. Keep scratching," I tell him. Tony digs in and Luna starts to lean in to his touch. She chokes out a cough and green alfalfa leaves spray out of her mouth. Then she licks her lips and swallows. Licks her lips and swallows. Drops her head and sighs.

"Turn on the water, please. Slow again." Paul turns on the hydrant. Rex places the hose against her face. Luna takes a long, loose breath and allows the water to seep into the deep crack along her forehead. The crusty pus starts to let free, one small chunk at a time until the larger chunks give way. I walk in closer to see the damage. I can see the bone. The edges of the skin around the break are already dead. Blood flow to this area has ceased long ago.

Sarah and Angie come up behind me and breathe heavy on the back of my neck as they stare at the damage. Luna's face looks like a topo map. Layers of pink, gray, and hints of green line the three-inch crack.

"Is she going to be okay?" Angie whispers.

I look around and see their faces leaning in toward Luna's pain.

"I don't know. Just keep the water coming." 🛡

INSCRIPTION ON A JEFFERSON DAVIS MONUMENT NEVER BUILT BUT MAYBE ONE DAY I WILL

North-facing side:

Charlie and I crossing
downtown, all the noise
and chaos, cold wind
pushing everything
back, crossing against
a black guy crossing
to the curb we just left
and he looks skeptical
at us as in head tilt question
eyes narrow thinking
and when we meet
close enough in the middle
he goes
how'd a white dude like you
end up with a beautiful
black boy like that
but smiles kind to let me
in on the joke, giving me
the setup of a vaudeville
routine never performed

but I don't know
my line—I got
the latest model, I
traded up, any attempt
at humor
disrespects the real
and I'm smiling
to let him know I get the joke
because sometimes it isn't
but I can't think
what to say
the universe aligns
its teeth into the grooves
of the other wheel
and turns
we're all hoofing it
fast with the wind and
traffic and we're past and
at the curb I look back
and he's moving on
and Charlie goes
do you know him
and I say no.

East-facing side:

There is a big wheel
that keeps turning.
To travel downriver
is to burn. Pumping
gas, cleaning plates,
there is a way
to be free, it sounds
like wind
catching a fire
and whipping it to frenzy,
there is a way to sing
that tells the story, it sounds
like screaming,
a cry
that's still
song. Big wheel
keep turning.

West-facing:

And I never lost a single
minute of sleep
worrying
about what might have been

South:

Does your child speak English?
Is your child Mexican?
Is your child Spanish?
Is your child oriental?
What country was he
born in? What do you know
about him? Have you ever heard
about the mother was
his father an athlete how long
did it take does he have
medical issues. What's the story
on the mom. Are you worried
about adjustment and problems. Let all
who gaze upon this stone
remember the valor and brazen charges
riding on into the mouth of hell
thundered an unanswered anthem
to the God of Battle—
Jefferson Davis Community College
in Brewton, Alabama, was founded
in 1964.

This is my monument
to Jefferson Davis.

NOME,
a Sonnet

Six huskies will be hitched along by dawn;

Embroidered on my coat, the village heads.

In perfect composition, one by one,
The townsmen knot their wishes to my sled.

They have no right to place their trust in me
For I have been ignored until, now sick,

They come to me as to them came disease—

And in that wake, my un-picked hand they pick.

I'll say of course that I am coming back
To harvest boon with any skull that's left;

But as I tie this Wolfsbane to my neck,

I take both traitor-breath, then hero-breath.
Departing past their patron eyes, I know:

"I'm leaving through these woods:
two lines in snow."

Mendelssohn

One summer when I was a boy, my father entered into a friendly rivalry with a giant raccoon, a creature that could dart across lawns as quietly as a house cat even though it was the size of a small refrigerator. The first attacks on our garbage cans began in June. Within weeks everyone in the neighborhood was so tired of retrieving their cans from where they'd been left dented in the street, of sweeping the remains of torn garbage bags from driveways and rooftops, of pulling swollen diapers and coffee filters from rain gutters, that all the usual small talk had been replaced by a single topic: a mutual hatred of the beast. For everyone, that is, except my father, who spoke of the vandalism with a peculiar admiration. Most adults in our neighborhood referred to the animal only as "the raccoon" or "that goddamned raccoon." It was my father who named him Mendelssohn.

Seth Fried

My sister, Olive, and I asked more than once why he settled on that name, but our father was a difficult person to understand when he was amusing himself. He would tell us that as a graduate student in Pittsburgh his upstairs neighbor had been a piano player who died suddenly or he would describe the color of the Elbe on a cloudy day in September when he had visited Germany as a boy.

The morning after an attack, it wasn't uncommon to catch Dad standing outside in his maroon bathrobe, his dark hair still messy from a night's sleep. He would be drinking coffee out of the Smurfs mug Olive and I had gotten him one year for Father's Day, chuckling to himself as he observed where Mendelssohn had wedged our neighbor's aluminum garbage can between the forked branches of the peeling birch tree in our front yard or where the creature had pulled our porch swing down into a ditch and halfheartedly tried to bury it. Dad would gamely carry the swing back up to our porch or grab a stepladder so he could pry the can out of the tree, all the while humming to himself what I would later recognize as the overture to Felix Mendelssohn's *A Midsummer Night's Dream*.

Our subdivision bordered farmland and Michigan wilderness, and so the garbage cans on our street had always been subject to the normal mischief of woodland pests. But on June 6, those of us on Oldberry Street woke to discover the evidence of an unprecedented level of animal-on-garbage violence. For a quarter mile on both sides of the street, cans were not only knocked over but in some cases bent in half and flattened. The garbage bags were all torn and piled twenty feet high in a greasy, dew-soaked mound in the middle of our street. Near the edges of the pile you could see the wet tire tracks where our neighborhood garbage truck, its driver adhering rigidly to the rules dictating the curbside presentation of refuse for collection, had slalomed around Mendelssohn's handiwork before continuing on his route.

By seven in the morning, every adult on Oldberry was staring up at the trash pile in horror. Olive and I still had two weeks of school left, but when we came down the stairs dressed for the day we found our parents standing in our open front door, Mom frowning at the egg-and-zoo stink that had begun to drift into the house. Olive nodded to me and we quickly returned to our bedrooms. Our unspoken policy whenever our parents were too distracted in the morning to make us go wait for the school bus was that neither of us should do anything to remind them of our presence in the house.

I watched the developing scene in the street from my bedroom window and Olive joined me after changing back into her pajamas. We crouched there with the window open and our chins on the sill, enjoying the adult confusion taking place below. That summer Olive was eleven and I was eight. In a few years my persistent boyishness combined with her sudden sense of maturity would begin to annoy her, but for the time being we were best friends.

In the street Mr. Butler was regarding the immensity of the mound and shouting about teenagers until Mrs. Lambert pointed to the gnawed garbage bags and conspicuous piles of feces surrounding the heap, loose scatter shots of cigarette-width turds. Olive supplied the voice for Mrs. Lambert, affecting a geriatric wobble as she did whenever she imitated an adult for my benefit, "Clarence, those aren't *teenager* droppings."

Mr. Wallace, our neighbor from across the street, squatted authoritatively over one of the scat piles and nodded in agreement with whatever Lambert's actual assessment had been. Wallace was a sixty-five-year-old retired gym teacher who had been on his way out for his morning run. He was tall and still athletic-looking, with a handlebar mustache and a head of white hair worn in a tight crew cut. His wife, also a retired teacher, had the same haircut and Olive had once observed that the mustache was essential in telling the two apart. They were ushers at St. Anthony's and had a habit of looking surprised that Dad never came to church with us. Earlier that year, they'd approached Mom after the service as we made our way out to the car. They asked her a few questions that seemed outwardly polite but that even to a child's ears were so freighted with strange undertones that on the ride home Olive asked what they had wanted.

"They think your dad is Jewish," Mom said.

"Why?"

"Because his last name is German," Mom said, sounding a little bored as she imagined our neighbors' suspicions. "And he has dark hair and doesn't go to Mass."

"He isn't though?" Olive said.

"No. He isn't anything. He's agnostic."

> By seven in the morning, every adult on Oldberry was staring up at the trash pile in horror.

Olive asked what that meant and Mom smiled, explaining that our father had taken one philosophy course in college and liked to sleep in on Sundays. At times she seemed to view our father's lack of religious obligation with a wistful jealousy bordering on pride, as if his ability to spend his Sunday mornings drinking coffee and reading P. G. Wodehouse novels was, to her, a kind of magic. After that Sunday at church, we would see Wallace stop whatever he was doing to stare at Dad whenever the two were outdoors at the same time. If Dad noticed, he didn't seem to care and would always smile at Wallace, giving him a friendly wave.

As Wallace examined the pile of droppings, he was bare-chested, wearing only a pair of blue track shorts and some ancient-looking gray sneakers. Olive and I were usually intimidated by the intensity of Mr. and Mrs. Wallace. But watching from my room, we felt more than comfortable laughing openly as he scrutinized that mound of feces as if it were a ransom note.

> At the mention of some kind of contagious worm everybody began to retreat.

"Raccoons," we heard him bray.

"Nobody touch it," he shouted, already up and jogging back to his garage. "It's poisonous."

Wallace's request that nobody touch the poop kept Olive and I cackling, but it was nothing compared to our reaction when we saw him walking confidently back down his driveway holding the homemade flamethrower he had once been in the habit of using to de-ice his driveway in the winter. A habit he stopped only after a few of our neighbors raised questions about its safety. As soon as everyone saw him with that yellow tank strapped to his back and the flame wand made from an old rifle stock with its pilot already lit, they all began to raise their voices in protest.

"Goddamnit, Donald," Mr. Emory said. "That's the last thing we need."

"No, *Stewart*," Wallace said, calling Emory by his first name as if it were an accusation itself, "the last thing we need is an outbreak of roundworm."

Emory looked around for a show of support from his neighbors, but at the mention of some kind of contagious worm everybody began to retreat into the safety of their lawns. Sighing, Emory trudged back to his own yard to watch from a safe distance as Wallace lit up the first pile.

The early morning sun shining on the wet garbage in the street was joined by the shifting light of Wallace's flamethrower as he walked from one pile of feces to the next. The mound of garbage flickered like a bonfire and Wallace's chest hair glowed a rosy orange. Olive and I held hands as we laughed. From my window we could see all the way to Elmer Road, where the school bus we were supposed to be on was floating by.

Unfortunately, the day's seeming perfection proved fleeting. Once Wallace was finished torching the rest of the raccoon droppings, everyone on our street banded together for a cleanup effort that included my sister and me, dashing our hopes of devoting our unexpected free day to our new favorite pastime of playing Beyond Castle Wolfenstein, just barely outsmarting 8-bit Nazis on the Apple II computer in our basement.

Instead we found ourselves putting on dishwashing gloves that went up to our elbows so we could wander around our yard picking up loose garbage. The only consolation was that the trash was a mix of everyone's, so the task of cleaning it up had what one might call a human interest element. Underneath the swing set in our backyard we found a deposit of empty prescription-medicine bottles, two pairs of men's underwear with the crotches worn out, and a long blond wig that was soaking wet. And so, during that day of yard work our parents heard no complaints from us.

The night before, Dad had forgotten to take our cans down to the curb, and so they had been locked in the wood-and-wire pen he had built behind our garage. Mendelssohn ripped the pen apart in order to get to our cans, so once the street was clear of trash Dad spent most of the day taking spare lumber from his woodshop in the garage to make the necessary repairs. He had been immensely proud of his garbage pen, as he was of anything he built, but he seemed to take its destruction in the spirit of constructive criticism. His expression as he stood over the tangle of wood and chicken wire in a pair of old jeans and his Cornell T-shirt was one of deepened focus, as if he were reevaluating the whole process of building a garbage pen in light of new and mysterious forces.

Dinner was almost over by the time he came back inside, smelling faintly of outdoors and body odor. Dad would have been the one to cook on any other night, but Mom had taken the day off work and was only too happy to throw something together while he kept himself busy. She said a project was good for his aimlessness, a word she used without judgment, as if she were describing a trick knee or a bad back. Our father, the aimless inventor. In his early twenties he had developed some sort of gas compressor and, as my mother put it, nobody in the country could build a decent refrigerator without having to cut him a check. But success had effectively retired him at the age of twenty-eight and Mom worried about his long periods of creative inactivity. As he sat down at the kitchen table, one could see that his mind was still far away in a land of reinforced joints, bolts, and epoxies. Eventually he wiped his face on the sleeve of his T-shirt and opened the can of Old Milwaukee Mom handed him.

"The pen lives," he said, smiling.

. . .

Wallace was the first to buy a pair of the pest-stopper garbage receptacles with clamping lids. They soon became a short-lived fad on our street since everyone still thought our neighborhood was dealing with an ordinary infestation of raccoons. One bright afternoon some of us also started to notice a few steel kill traps glittering in Wallace's lawn. It was Mrs. Nowak, a proud owner of two outdoor tabby cats and a sandy blond cocker spaniel named Futz, who publicly urged Wallace to replace those lethal measures with the humane kennel traps that could be seen all over our neighborhood with campfire marshmallows and lumps of wet cat food sitting on their bait plates. He eventually made a show of acquiescing, but those of us who lived nearby saw that he just moved the kill traps to his backyard.

Ours was the only house not to put out any traps at all. Because of Dad's faith in his reconstructed pen, he wouldn't even consent to buying any of the special pest-proof cans. His plan was to wake up early on collection days and take our old, metal cans to the curb once the truck was making its way down our street. And so, each house embracing its own level of preparedness, the neighborhood waited.

Two weeks later Mrs. Rubio went into her backyard to replenish her bird feeder and discovered that her aboveground pool had been filled with garbage, the mound of bags bobbing on the water and spilling over onto the pool's wooden deck. Also, Mrs. Rubio's bird feeder, a miniature Victorian gazebo atop a five-foot-tall aluminum pole, had been yanked out of the ground and was never seen again.

The rest of the neighborhood hadn't fared much better. The pest-proof receptacles had presented Mendelssohn with some difficulty, but only in the sense that the lids remained fastened and he was forced to bite through the middle of the cans, pulling the bags out through grapefruit-sized holes. He left a trail of toppled cans down our street, all of them looking like wounded soldiers with their guts tumbling out. After several houses he seemed to get the hang of this new method, nearly chewing the cans in half before plucking out the bags.

The majority of the stolen trash wound up in the Rubio pool, though some was also wedged into a half dozen or so of the humane cage traps. At first this appeared to be a maneuver to remove the trap's bait without the trick door locking into place, but in all instances the bait was left untouched, except for the few cases in which it had been defecated upon. Wallace most likely would have viewed the failure of those cages as a moral victory if it weren't for the fact that three of his hidden kill traps had also been found by the animal and flung into his prized rosebushes. The traps had clapped shut on impact, mangling the flowers.

When Dad stepped outside early that morning, he was dumbfounded to find that his new and improved pen had been pulled up and dragged a good thirty feet into our backyard, where our empty garbage cans were all tipped over and scattered. He joined us at the breakfast table, a distant look on his face as he told us there had been another attack. He was still leaning back in a kitchen chair with his mouth

> He left a trail of toppled cans down our street, all of them looking like wounded soldiers.

hanging open when Mrs. Davis rang the bell to tell Mom what had happened to the Rubio family pool. With her strong sense of community, Mom sent Olive and me to the garage to get what were now our designated garbage-handling gloves, instructing us to volunteer at the Rubios' while she and Dad cleaned up our yard.

Olive and I were anxious to get a close look at the garbage-filled pool, but when we got there the oldest Rubio boy, Stephen, told us to stay out of the way. We pressed ourselves against their back fence and watched as several men from the neighborhood brought up sopping wet garbage bags while Stephen and his younger brother, Velmer, used pool skimmers to fish out sheets of newspaper and paper towels that had become as elusive as ribbons of seaweed. The men were careful to check the bags for tears before pulling them out, keeping the holes closed with one hand as they hoisted the bags out with the other. But as Mr. Conklin lifted up one particularly overstuffed bag, he failed to notice a long rip down its side. The bag emptied itself into the water, filling the pool with an orange-and-brown mush. Everyone present groaned in frustration. As a large island of mush bobbed gradually away from Mr. Conklin, he occupied himself with a series of heartfelt *fucks* and *goddamnits*.

But to my own surprise, my happy contemplation of the scene was interrupted by the dawning of a thought I found somewhat unsettling.

"At breakfast," I said to Olive, "did you see Dad's face?"

"I know," she said. "I don't think I've ever seen him that happy."

I kept my eyes on the pool without saying anything, but I understood what she meant.

Dad's astonishment at the destruction of his improved pen had betrayed a strange sense of excitement on his part that bothered me if only because it was so unfamiliar. My father was always happy and energetic, but astounded? Thrilled? No. I'm now older than my father was that summer by six months and looking back I can tell you that he was a pleasant man with nothing to prove, someone to whom financial success and a warm family life had come unnaturally easy. As a result, it was often impossible to ignore his sweet boredom. Dad washing dishes by hand in the kitchen, whistling something by Jethro Tull. Dad, unseen, moving boxes in the garage for hours without explanation. Dad wondering aloud at the dinner table if it'd be difficult to learn Japanese. Until the presence of Mendelssohn, I hadn't realized how comforting I'd found our father's quiet restlessness.

> Those who could afford it installed chain link rodent fences and floodlights on timers.

After a while we returned home to find our own yard already clear of trash. Stepping through the front door, Olive reported that we had been dismissed from pool-cleaning duty with the heartfelt thanks of the Rubio family, a claim that went unscrutinized since my parents were busy carrying my father's heavy oak drafting table up from his cluttered workspace in the basement. We watched from the top of the stairs and Mom smiled up at us.

"Your father wants to work in the family room," she said before blowing a strand of hair out of her face.

Mom was ambitious by nature. She was a business reporter for the *Free Press* and whenever she saw that a story of hers had gotten bumped to page one, we would find her standing in the foyer wearing a tank top and a pair of Dad's boxer shorts, pointing at her byline and saying, "You're goddamn right." Likewise, she had a great enthusiasm for my father's abilities and seemed anxious, after his many years of idleness, for him to once again put them to use.

They arranged the table in our family room so it faced the large sliding glass doors that looked out onto our backyard. Just outside you could see where Dad had carefully disassembled his pen, its materials stacked on the patio. He went back down to the basement to fetch his drafting chair and some supplies. When he returned, he filled the table's built-in cubbies with mechanical pencils, gummy erasers, engineering scales, and masking tape, at which point Mom finally asked him what it was he'd be working on.

"Raccoons," he said, taking a seat and taping a piece of plotter paper to the desk's slanted surface.

"Racoons," she repeated.

She wasn't asking for clarification, just making sure she'd heard him correctly.

He adjusted his stool and nodded.

"It's an interesting problem."

She smiled down at him, watching him start to draw, eventually taking his free hand and kissing it.

• • •

The rest of the neighborhood lacked my father's ingenuity, and so as Mendelssohn's attacks continued many families found themselves at a loss. Neither the traps nor the special garbage cans had worked and animal control was known to be useless unless you had something cornered in your garage. Some neighbors began to meet with consultants from pest control companies, most of whom were dismissed as soon as they launched into their pitches featuring glossy photographs of the same humane catch-and-release traps and secure garbage cans that had already proved so ineffective. Those who could afford it installed chain link rodent fences and floodlights on timers. The Ronaldsons even purchased a set of outdoor speakers that were supposed to drive pests away with special high frequencies. Wallace could be seen putting a lot of work into his yard, but other than the heavy wire cages he'd placed over some of his more delicate plants, it was difficult to tell what our most reactionary neighbor's plan was when it came to defending his home.

Meanwhile, Dad had begun conducting interviews with our neighbors and was starting to hypothesize—weeks before the first sighting—that our neighborhood wasn't dealing with a normal infestation of pests but the efforts of a single, genius raccoon. He hung a corkboard next to his drafting table and pinned to it the Polaroids he had taken of the damage he'd observed at the homes of those he interviewed. In the photographs you could see his hand holding up a yellow pocket ruler to bite marks left in garbage cans and aluminum siding. He did the same with any paw prints he could find, noting not only their size but also the fact that they all seemed to be coming from the same animal. That was around the time we first started to hear the name Mendelssohn, Dad dropping it into conversation as if we had all already agreed it was the creature's name.

Through the course of his research, he quickly became dissatisfied with our public library's lack of adult nonfiction devoted to the subject of raccoons. He ended up driving to Detroit one weekend to wander the high, plentiful stacks of the downtown branch. He returned in the evening holding a single leather-bound book containing a text from the late eighteenth century. It was in French and titled *Le journal d'Etienne Boudin, un coureur de bois.*

Dad said his French was a little *rouillé*, and so it took him some time to translate the text. He spent hours flipping back and forth through a French to English dictionary, lurching his way through Boudin's beautiful and discursive views on the subject of raccoons. He recorded his translation on a yellow legal pad and would follow us around the house, reading passages aloud to anyone who'd listen. Boudin described a boar raccoon climbing headfirst down a tree as "moving cautiously with the weight of his own body, hands outstretched, half pleading, half curious. A man feeling his way through a darkened room." A sow raccoon placed Juneberries in her mouth with an expression in her eyes "as if she had knowledge of a joke yet to be told." When Dad recited these passages, his voice came out bewildered, as if these poetic descriptions of nature's proud burglars contained truths so essential and beautiful that they were wounding him. The corkboard became crowded with quotes from Boudin's book, lines describing the chirping of raccoons as "panicked but playful," and their silence as being "colder than the light of the moon."

Dad was also delighted to discover a formula the old trapper had developed for determining the size of creatures through an analysis of their paw prints. The calculation took into account not only the length, width, and depth of the print but also the quality of the soil, which Boudin had differentiated into over two hundred basic types: dry dark loam, dark loam within two days of heavy rain, river silt during two weeks of drought, etc. Using this model and the various photographs he had taken, Dad estimated Mendelssohn to be three feet long and around 105 pounds.

"Yowza," Mom said, when he reported his finding at dinner. "So it really is a monster raccoon?"

"Well, 'monster' seems a little strong," he said, placing a hand on the pile of notes he had brought with him to the table.

"He's not"—he had to search for the word—"he's not *usual*, if that's what you mean."

However, Boudin had been a trader of furs, and so the traps he described were all decidedly lethal. The formula Dad had used to determine the animal's size was followed in the text by a chart explaining the corresponding size of boulder that would be needed to crush that animal's skull, but Dad was insistent that killing the creature was out of the question. After all, he was fond of pointing out, he was incapable of *building* a raccoon. No. Mendelssohn could be stopped only with compassion and sportsmanship.

Dad estimated Mendelssohn to be three feet long and around 105 pounds.

While studying Boudin's design for a deadfall, Dad came up with what he referred to as a livefall. After consulting with Mom, he dug a large hole in our backyard, filling it with metal tracks, wiring, and some spring hinges. When he was finished there was a platform of perforated metal in the middle of our backyard that was eight feet long by six feet wide and level with the grass. If weight in the center of the platform increased by forty pounds or more, the platform dropped at mousetrap speed and assembled itself into a large cage, which could then be pulled out of the ground.

Dad couldn't stop smiling as he demonstrated its operation. He did so a dozen times by pushing on the platform with the handle of a rake as Olive and I watched. The inner workings of the trap were so efficient that it barely made a noise, just a faint click and a soft flourish like an umbrella being opened. He had designed the trap to accommodate a raccoon the size of a sheepdog, but he still worried that it might maim the creature if it wasn't calibrated just right. Eventually he went into the garage to take from the deep freeze one of the birthday cakes he'd purchased for bait, placing it on my skateboard and rolling it to the middle of the platform. If the cake survived the trap he said we could celebrate by having it for dessert that night, and so Olive and I watched with an air of serious appraisal as he pressed on the platform once more with the rake's handle, the cake's red and blue flowers of frosting looking fragile and alert. A breeze hissed through the grass, but otherwise the backyard was quiet. When the cake finally disappeared into the livefall and came back up without so much as a bruised petal, Olive and I screamed and jostled each other.

With the trap a success, Dad spent a week determining when Mendelssohn would strike again. He worked late into the night, pouring over Boudin's observations. He consulted his own hand-drawn maps of our neighborhood, weather reports, calendars on which he had penciled in the phases of the moon. His calculations went on until July 2, when he went out to the deep freeze to get another cake. It sat on the platform of the livefall from the early evening on, bright white under an overcast sky. He gave us all his word that Mendelssohn would strike that night and he wasn't wrong.

> Dad didn't say a word, just walked toward Wallace with purpose and punched him in the mouth.

• • •

Mom protested when Dad mentioned a stakeout. The plan was for him to sit in our family room all night with the lights off, keeping an eye on Mendelssohn's cake out in the backyard. Mom had already spoken to him about the irregular hours he had been keeping and that night the strained patience in her voice suggested she might be worried that her husband was taking his interest in a local raccoon a bit too seriously. But the look of happy determination in his eyes won her over and she ended up starting the coffeemaker for him before heading upstairs to bed.

His family asleep upstairs, he sat drinking coffee with Yoo-hoo in it. He had rigged a floodlight to turn on once the livefall was triggered and to this day I like to imagine him sitting there expectantly, waiting to be blinded by his own success. Instead, around two in the morning he was startled by three loud rifle reports and the sound of one of our front windows being shattered.

As it turned out, my father wasn't the only one on our street waiting for Mendelssohn to return. Ever since Mr. Wallace's rosebushes were mangled, he had been dressing up in a black sweat suit a few nights a week and hiding behind those same bushes with a pair of night vision goggles and a hunting rifle. According to his account of the night's events, which our family learned later through neighborhood gossip, Mendelssohn had been trotting down our street with a large white garbage bag in his mouth. The bag was overfull, but Mendelssohn dragged it along at a brisk pace, leaving a wet trail of grease on the pavement. Wallace was shocked not only by Mendelssohn's size but also by his strange coloring, all black with a narrow white streak across his eyes. Wallace must have made a little too much noise as he adjusted his grip on his rifle because Mendelssohn dropped the bag from his mouth and turned to face the rosebush containing our neighbor. Wallace aimed quickly and fired, his first shot grazing the creature. Instead of fleeing, Mendelssohn charged at Wallace, who let off another two shots, one of which went through our first-story window. By then lights all along our street flicked on and Mendelssohn, perhaps sensing himself outnumbered, dashed in a black streak toward our backyard.

When Dad realized the sound of broken glass had come from our house, he rushed upstairs to make sure we were all safe. He found me sitting up in bed and pulled back my covers, patting at my chest and stomach. He ignored my confused, middle-of-the-night questions and examined my arms one at a time before kissing my forehead and rushing down the hall.

While he was making sure Mom and Olive were safe, I opened my bedroom window and watched as Wallace stood in front of his driveway. His rifle was now leaning against his garage door as he addressed a group of our startled-looking neighbors. When he demonstrated the size of the creature with his hands, the people on our street finally started to seem more curious than upset and drew in closer to hear what he had to say. That was when I heard my father thunder down our steps on his way out the front door.

Wallace turned from his audience and raised his palm to Dad as he approached.

"I'll have your window fixed," he said, his tone suggesting that any complaints my father had were sure to be trivial.

Dad didn't say a word, just walked toward Wallace with purpose and punched him in the mouth. Wallace's eyes went wide and he grabbed Dad by the collar of his sweat shirt as if he were about to scold a child. Dad hit him a second time and the two men stumbled away from each other.

A woman in the crowd screamed and some men moved to stop Dad without daring to touch him. Wallace was stooped over, holding his mouth and staring up at Dad with what looked like genuine hate. Dad stepped back from the crowd and pointed at our open front door, a wild tremor in his hand.

"My family lives in that house," he shouted. "My family lives in that house, you goddamned animals."

He waited for someone to understand what he meant before hollering even louder, *"Call the police!"*

Inside, Mom collected Olive and me, ordering us into her and Dad's bed. Then she went out to calm Dad down so he wouldn't be arrested once somebody from the sheriff's department showed up. Fortunately, the young deputy who arrived spent most of his time talking Dad and Wallace out of pressing charges. After the deputy climbed back into his cruiser, Dad noticed a light coming from our backyard. He ran to check on the livefall, but when he pulled up the cage it was empty except for the grocery store cake, a single print on top and a plum-sized divot out of its side where Mendelssohn had had just enough time to grab a single pawful.

An hour later we were all in my parents' bed. I rested my cheek against Dad's arm and he put it around me before letting out a long, disappointed sigh.

· · ·

The next day Olive and I were unimpressed as we rode our bikes around the neighborhood. Mendelssohn had been interrupted in his work and so there were only a half-dozen mangled cans along our street. We stopped in front of the Conklin house and the sight of Mr. Conklin sweeping up a modest spill of toilet paper tubes and soda bottles in his driveway seemed especially pathetic after Mendelssohn's previous acts of destruction. We were just about to abandon our tour of the neighborhood when Pat Drexler squealed up on his bike. Drexler was a boy my age with a blond flattop and an assertive way of talking that made it difficult for me to tell whether he was trying to bully or befriend me.

"I heard your dad went crazy last night," he said.

Olive had been about to pedal off, but at the word "crazy" she lowered one foot back down to the street.

"Mr. Wallace could have killed us," she said.

Drexler wiped his nose on his shoulder.

"My dad says your dad's scared 'cause Jews don't believe in heaven."

I thought about this for a second.

"People who believe in heaven want to get shot?"

Olive put her hand on my shoulder as a signal that I wasn't helping.

"Our dad isn't Jewish," she said.

Drexler regarded us with a blank, open stare.

"My mom says there's nothing wrong with being Jewish. It's part of your heritage."

He looked around impatiently before pedaling away, anxious to have this same conversation about our father's Semitic rage with anyone he could find.

On the ride back to our house, Olive shook her head and called Drexler an idiot. Otherwise, we were both quiet. Neither of us had anything against the idea of our father being Jewish. We had no idea what that would even mean, but the strange curiosity and insistence of our neighbors gave it all the force of an accusation.

> He waited for someone to understand what he meant before hollering even louder, *"Call the police!"*

I was too young to have words for any of this at the time, but my grade school education had already instilled in me the single piece of wisdom it had to offer, which was that being different was dangerous, and so there was a queasy feeling in my stomach as I thought about what Drexler had said. Olive seemed more troubled by his naïve oversimplification regarding non-Christians and the afterlife, which had perhaps played into preexisting concerns that our father never came with us to Mass, where eternal hellfires were mentioned as matter-of-factly as bake sales and spaghetti dinners.

When Dad returned from the hardware store later that afternoon with a new pane of glass, Olive marched up to him as he was coming through the door and asked him if he believed in heaven. He stopped where he was and adjusted his grip on the pane, which was wrapped in a white foam sheet. He looked confused, giving Olive the same friendly shrug we gave him whenever he asked us what we had learned at school that day. But when Olive continued to look concerned, his face turned serious, finally breaking into a sweet smile when he thought he understood.

"Don't worry, Ollie," he said. "Mendelssohn's not dead."

She tried to rearticulate the question, but Dad was walking the glass sideways into our living room and telling us to make ourselves useful. Mom had made him promise that he would fix the window and the part of our living room wall where Wallace's bullet had lodged itself before he got into any more raccoon business, so now he was briskly carrying out the task with Olive and me as his assistants. We handed him the heat gun, the putty knife, and the can of linseed oil while he talked about the paw prints in the bait cake and the absence of blood near the livefall. He cited both as prime evidence that Mendelssohn had survived Wallace's ambush, which he described as both cowardly and uninspired.

"His idea of solving the crossword puzzle," Dad said, pushing on the sash to make sure the window was secure, "is to light the newspaper on fire."

Despite Wallace's recklessness, he enjoyed some celebrity as Mendelssohn's presumed killer.

The more he spoke on the subject, the clearer it became that his plan was no longer just to capture Mendelssohn, but to find some way to save him from harm.

Olive had been silent after he misunderstood her question, but her interest seemed to be piqued by the way he spoke of Mendelssohn. I had already decided to ignore our strange conversation with Drexler and was anxious for Dad to finish his repairs so Olive and I could go play computer games in the basement. But Olive was still grappling with something and, as she listened to Dad talk about Mendelssohn with nothing but love and concern, it appeared to be subtly undoing whatever anxiety Drexler had inspired in her.

After the pane was installed and the bullet hole spackled, Olive was suddenly unenthusiastic about our plans to spend the rest of the day on the Apple II. Halfway through her turn she stopped just short of shooting a Nazi. She was captured and the screen read, "They got you!"

Before I could tell her where she'd gone wrong, she stood up and violated our cardinal rule by unplugging the Apple II to turn it off.

"Olive! What's your problem?"

"Come on," she said, in a voice I would hear more and more often in the years to come, when she possessed such a sure authority that it was as if she herself were only responding to orders that were of distant and mysterious origin. "We're helping Dad."

Despite Wallace's recklessness, he enjoyed some celebrity as Mendelssohn's presumed killer. Neighbors stopped by his house in the evening with thank-you gifts, stepping inside for beer and coffee to hear him tell of his encounter with the creature. This newfound popularity was cut short after a few days, when Mendelssohn struck our neighborhood again in full force. After arranging another massive garbage mound on Wood Street, he pulled down an entire tree house in which the Campario twins had accidentally left a box of Oatmeal Creme Pies.

Our father woke us early that morning with the good news.

"Mendelssohn's back," he shouted from the bottom of the stairs.

As part of our participation in Dad's new plan, Olive and I had received special dispensation to sleep in our clothes, and so all we had to do was grab our notebooks and shoes before heading out to get our first look at Mendelssohn's carnage. As we tied our sneakers, I was full of a boyish sense of adventure, while Olive frowned seriously down at her white Keds.

"Double-check everything you write down," she said. "We have to be positive what he eats."

Dad had given us separate routes around the neighborhood to patrol on our bikes while he investigated on foot. Together the three of us were able to survey the damage quickly before any cleanup efforts could obscure the trail of evidence that Mendelssohn had left behind. The first page of my notebook had a checklist in my father's handwriting, composed of over thirty observations calibrated to determine how Mendelssohn had spent his time at each house:

· *Cans destroyed or just knocked over?*
· *Bags ripped open or just pulled out?*
· *Bags tossed into the yard, street, or missing?*

After collecting data from a handful of attacks, Dad's analysis was that Mendelssohn was drawn to a perfect trifecta of garbage on Spring Street, where the Lamberts with their five cats produced bags filled with stale cat food and used kitty litter, while just across the street was the Ronson family, whose patriarch was a notorious yo-yo dieter who made no secret of the fact that he tended to buy sweets and guiltily throw them away half eaten. Next to the Ronsons were the Vesuvios, who had three teenage daughters and their two-year-old miracle baby, Andy, meaning their garbage was a pungent combination of full diapers, used sanitary napkins, discarded cosmetics, and a fine mash of wet Nilla wafers and Cheerios. These three houses provided a cocktail of waste that Mendelssohn found irresistible.

Having arrived at this conclusion, we moved on to the next phase of the plan, which involved going on a few late-night garbage raids, stealing bags from the trifecta houses, and storing them in airtight rubber bins in our garage. Mom had been nothing but supportive up to that point, but as Dad slid yet another bin of our neighbors' trash under the large woodworking bench in the garage, he said it was probably best that we not trouble her with this aspect of our project.

Next he set his sights on the undeveloped strip of land we owned that extended a half acre beyond our back fence. It was a few dozen trees on a gentle slope leading down to a shallow creek. After clearing some brush, he gave me and Olive shovels and had us dig a pond for Mendelssohn to defile in the same manner as the Rubio pool. Dad also used the dirt we displaced to fashion the type of generic animal den that Boudin claimed raccoons were fond of taking over for themselves. He mixed the dirt with water and an organic fixative of his own design, applying the mixture to a metal frame he'd built that was the size and shape of a round camping tent. The frame contained a network of wires and pressure sensors and air vents made from PVC pipe, all of which he worked quickly to cover over with mud, not talking unless he was giving us instructions.

He had reason to hurry. After receiving a record number of calls, trucks from animal control were now patrolling our neighborhood on a regular basis. And during a trip to Johnson's Independent Hardware to get some spring hinges and wire connectors, Dad had spotted Wallace in the hunting department. The sheriff's deputy had warned Wallace against discharging any firearms in the neighborhood, and so at Johnson's he was holding a crossbow bolt up to the light and smiling at its black point as if it were the glint in a diamond.

Olive emulated Dad's intensity as we worked in the woods and shushed me when I marveled at a giant worm my shovel had unearthed. I held it up for her to see as it curled and groped in the open air. I was more confused than hurt when she kept her eyes down and told me to keep digging. Her seriousness had already made the digging seem more like a chore and now that I'd officially been bossed I thought about asking if I could go back inside. But then it occurred to me that once Mendelssohn was captured our summer could go back to normal, Olive and me shunning another too-bright summer day in the cool, dark basement, eating bologna sandwiches and potato chips in front of the computer while Mom wrote in the kitchen and Dad sat with his feet up in the living room, reading some fat, sun-faded paperback. In other words, I kept digging.

By the time we finished filling in our freshly dug pond with buckets of creek water, Dad's mud den had dried. It was a hideous, lump-ridden mound, but sturdy, something he tested by taking a sledgehammer from the garage and striking it a few times with all his strength. The den's entrance let out the dull rubber *boing* of a hollow tire being struck.

The noise seemed to please him and he moved his tools to our back fence, where he mounted an electrical box with a bundle of wires snaking out of it and leading back to the den. He waited a few days, until his calculations predicted Mendelssohn would attack again, then he loaded the garbage bags we had stolen from our neighbors into the den like an offering, topping off the pile of garbage with another cake. That night the animal control trucks were out late. They rolled down our street one at a time in slow, solitary patrols, their headlights filling our house with waves of yellow light as they passed. The occasional squeal of their brakes made it difficult to sleep, as did the suspicion that Wallace was out there hiding with his crossbow, waiting for any sign of the precocious creature that was under my father's protection.

> There was a heavy thumping sound coming from the den, followed by a low, loud growl.

By early the next morning our neighborhood was untouched but there was a lively, almost peppery stench coming from our backyard. Dad woke Olive and me and the three of us ran barefoot toward the source of the reek.

He opened the electrical box on our fence with a key he took from the pocket of his bathrobe and carefully examined a pressure meter dangling inside. After blinking his sleep-swollen eyes at the meter, he flipped a black plastic switch inside the box. From the trees there was a metallic clank as the secret hatch my father had built into the mouth of the den swung shut. Soon, there was a heavy thumping sound coming from the den, followed by a low, loud growl. The power of Mendelssohn's complaints caused the distance between us and the den to shrink and a rush of fear moved through us as if we had just caught the universe by its tail.

Only after this frightened moment passed did we all think to celebrate our victory with a cheer that caused dogs two and three houses away to start howling.

"All right," Dad said, once our shouts died down.

He looked out to where the den could just be glimpsed through the trees, the low mound shaking and hopping in the dirt from the force of Mendelssohn's blows. "Now comes the tricky part."

· · ·

Dad got dressed and spent the rest of the morning on the phone in our kitchen, haggling over rental fees. In a few hours a flatbed truck rolled up onto our lawn followed soon after by a truck bearing a fifty-foot crane. Olive and I buzzed around him, asking him what was happening, but he was busy waving both vehicles into our backyard. Once they were in position, four large men in dirty blue coveralls stepped down from the cabs. They looked intimidating until they heard the animal wails coming from the tree line and started to exchange nervous looks with one another. As Dad led them back into the woods to show them how to attach the crane's cable to the hidden hitch loop he'd installed in the den's roof, they all held bandanas over their mouths to handle the stench. When they reached the den, one of them was forced to turn away for a moment to give in to a dry heave.

> The monstrous thumps had been replaced by the sound of light, searching scratches.

Olive and I watched from the family room as the cable went taut and the den was lifted from the ground. Dad shouted instructions and encouragement to the crew, applauding like a nervous coach as they hustled into position beneath the descending den. It swung pendulously through the air on its way to the awaiting flatbed, jerking to one side every few seconds from Mendelssohn throwing himself against its walls. Once the den came to rest, the crew had to work quickly to secure it before Mendelssohn's struggling could topple it from the truck bed. After they covered it with a blue tarp, Dad came inside and seemed surprised to see us still in our pajamas.

"Get dressed," he said. "We're going on a trip."

With the crane and its crew departed, our family loaded ourselves into the flatbed's roomy cab. Pulling around the side of our house, we saw

Wallace standing in the middle of his lawn, watering his grass with a limp gurgle from his garden hose. Mendelssohn was still mewling loudly and Wallace squinted at us, looking too confused by the whole scene to disapprove. As Dad turned right onto Oldberry, he gave Wallace a neighborly wave.

That day there was a great deal of music, a few deftly played rounds of the alphabet game, and the passing of sandwiches from the cooler at my mother's feet with an efficiency that became a point of pride for all of us. After driving north all day and most of that night, Dad pulled the truck to the side of the road just outside Traverse City, near a thick stretch of woods that loomed above the open rows of a black cherry orchard.

When Dad cut the engine, we could hear Mendelssohn's complaints again. His fierce growl was now a soft moan and the monstrous thumps coming from inside the den had been replaced by the sound of light, searching scratches. We all stayed in the truck while Dad left to climb up onto the bed. He threw off the tarp and pressed on a hidden panel so the den's small hatch sprang open. He took a step back and there was a long, still moment.

Mom, Olive, and I were huddled against the cab's rear window, trying to see anything moving in the darkness of the open hatch. Then, in a wave of black fur, Mendelssohn leapt out onto the truck bed and off into the grass, landing with barely a sound, before coursing dark and huge toward the far trees. Mom and Olive hugged.

I was happy too. Because Mendelssohn had been gotten rid of so humanely, I felt we had earned the right to spend the rest of our summer in an air of undisturbed bliss. Life, I told myself, could finally go back to the way it was meant to be. But it seemed to surprise Olive and Mom when I jokingly shouted, "Good riddance!"

Meanwhile, Dad had climbed on top of the den, where he gave out a loud whoop. He gave another and then leaned forward, resting his hands on his knees like a man catching his breath. The light from the road was behind him and his face was in shadow. When he shook, he could have been laughing or crying. It was a hot night, so as he climbed back into the cab I couldn't tell if his face was just damp with sweat. The serene look on his face offered no clues. He closed the driver's side door with a chipper bang, kissed Mom, and then looked down at the wheel of the truck in front of him as if it were a suggestion.

"Okay," he said, nodding and reaching for the ignition, "okay."

That night, we stayed in a roadside motel and didn't get back home until late the next day. After we pulled into our driveway, I jumped down from the cab of the truck and told Olive I'd race her to the Apple II. She had been quiet the whole trip home and told me she was too tired to play, a feeling of embarrassment seeming to spring up between us at my childish excitement.

In the months and years to come, the frequency of moments like that increased so gradually that I'm not even sure when the Olive I was best friends with was gone. Though, I've never once stopped expecting I might see her again. It's a kind of faith or stubbornness that I like to think I got from Dad. For example, he could never admit that Mendelssohn must have died at some point. Decades later when Dad was in the hospital for the last time—Mom smiling at him from her chair and holding his hand while Olive talked authoritatively with the nurses and I stood at the foot of his bed in my winter coat looking as though I'd just been slapped—he was chatting about how we had all saved Mendelssohn's life. His voice was a croak, almost unrecognizable, but he talked about Mendelssohn as if he were still way up north, drinking from the cool water of creeks and munching on the dropped fruit of now-overgrown orchards, the tartness of the cherries making the animal's eyes water in gratitude and the apples, soft from the fall, almost too sweet to bear. 🔯

HUNTER

Erotic dancing takes the place of Greek tragedy
just as the gladiatorial fights did in Rome—but it is a
private dance
no one can touch or see. A feeling every day I enter and close
a curtain behind. Sitting alone with it,
looking at it through a tiny hole,
something lithe and naked, shaking in the spotlight
beyond which I can never reach—

suffering cannot do what it did for Christ.
We do not get to go home afterward, cannot be
imagined into the arms of the absent father. See how
I do not rise up or shift the stone, do not
inspire a nation—I sit at the bar
consuming fried food. I put $5 into a machine
and shoot bucks with a long green rifle,
not speaking, not calling out anyone's name,
just me and the deer
grazing in a digital clearing of the wood.

I can't tell anymore for whom I grieve.
Something bigger

and more catastrophic has died
but died out of necessity—something that thought itself
into *indispensability*
something burst from every atom
outward, like autumn fireworks over the lake
and now
I'm just recording its scream and glitter-down,
just making a serial
from its fantastical, dazzling demise—
I can't tell anymore whether I am grieving *you* particularly
or I simply find life and death erroneous—this
big expired grief
             like a limb people deny ownership of, find
in their beds and throw on the floor, only to be told
      again and again, when the
whole body is thrown with it—that it is

attached,

      it is theirs, that they were
born with it.

INTERIOR DESIGN

How fabulous that humans are able to decorate from their minds. In
    a sense, they splatter their brains on the walls, translate texture
    from the head onto objects; carve into the very tusk, chisel onto the
    veranda, sew into quilts and lay them over the bodies of guests.

And what joy I get from that. From *décor*. From personal flair.
(Just look at the detail! Velvet. Chintz. Oak. Mint-condition. Patina.
    Hand-stitched . . .)
Even an absence of objects reflects a certain taste.

    *

I hold court all day on my own intellectual shortcomings.
It doesn't matter anymore. I'm led through hallways
into blue and gold vestiges
of the old rue Saint-Thomas-du-Louvre
and the historic apartments that adorned it.
I enter the rank beauty of my women's homes:
the familiar minute details of hoarding; draperies
in mixed scenes of toile, Venetian lamps, boxes, endless mail,
vases large enough to hold a child, filled with flowers
on their last legs, scattering the perfume of almost-decay.

I rendezvous in the living room with Mom.
I feel like your rejection slips, collated in a folder. Outdated science
    magazine
of inaccurate information—
I would love to "move on." But I carry you around like a scar,
forgetting sometimes that it is even there
until I follow a stranger's eye to it during a handshake.

*

My father-in-law keeps his wife's ashes in a tiny silver golf bag around his
    neck.
His favorite word is *nice*. When the service is "nice," the world makes
    sense.
If I could, I'd have kept a nice bone from your hand,
a notch of your middle finger, or a long clavicle; your whole skull . . .
But I would not have kept ashes.

Ashes remind me of my childhood—
shoveling them into a metal bucket from the wood stove
and sneaking them across the road
to dump in the cow field—Mom crying out for a load of wood
on my way back in—to me, ashes are too
anonymous.

*

Ah, so posh, so tasteful in grief. Some aesthetic leftover from the Greeks
mingled with the late booty of colonialism.
It fills me with a sense of leadership just being among the collected, the amassed,
the eccentric.

If I were to make a banner for my House it might be
a gray owl with its talons outstretched,
a 1989 Toyota broken down on the side of the road,
a blue jay in the center field of black wheat stalks,
a woman's silhouette at the center of a pentagram—
my flag would be so Metal, so Hardcore,
with a touch of *the feminine, beaux esprits.*
Something of gallantry,
integrity, and science, all wrapped up in one emblematic clutch—

Nothing was ever "nice" in my family.
They bear an intensity that allows
only for extremes:

      It's always been either "You're a *genius*!"
Or "You're a Hitler."

MY GIFT

I run around the block eating an orange & drop
its rind in continents on concrete. This is my gift
to the suburb, which told me not to burn logs

when the air quality is marked yellow. My dog
chases me around the block barking, & a woman
yells from her portrait window she could sue me

for not using a leash. My phone reminds me to take
a shower, so I do. It's not that I'm dirty, it's that
I'd rather stay in bed wearing fur, watching

documentaries about Dior. I apologize to no one
while scrubbing my scalp until it bleeds. I know
what it is to stare at yourself in a shattered mirror

& not remember if it was you who broke it.
I wanted to see if I could mine my body for rubies,
& look, I can! I write a letter & don't send it:

Here is a book & a ruby. One from my body,
the other I made after a fit with a pen. Both
worth nothing, but I like the thought of a man
picking them up & holding them in his hands.

FOR MY SON BORN IN LA MARISCAL
—Ciudad Juárez

You bob & spit & bite
    at my breast. You are my private
colony of sharp stones. I burn
    your umbilical cord to ash.
Come, meet the spirits. Before
    your birth I thought you an eyeball
bruised purple. I have no crib
    to leave you in, but a maizena cardboard box
& a blanket of my thick dark hair.
    I have done many things to feed your body—
open-legged, dark-thumbed
    things. Things for the price of what I
can endure in thirty minutes before
    breaking. I know I can't keep you,
but even stillborn I used the blood
    I gave you to wash my legs clean.

WON'T BACK DOWN

ON ROBERT SHEA AND
ROBERT ANTON WILSON'S

The Illuminatus! Trilogy

JOHN FISCHER

I first came into possession of *The Illuminatus! Trilogy*, in its staggering 805-page glory, at a hobby shop in central Long Island. This was during my middle school years,

when a weekend playing "tabletop strategy games" and eating cold pizza seemed like the ideal use of my time. The hobby shop, Men at Arms, attracted what I now understand to be a kind of nerd paramilitary crowd: men in cargo pants who knew the unreported details of the Oklahoma City bombing and the effective range of 5.56 mm ammunition. Larry, an old British goth in a leather trench coat, lent me a copy of *The Illuminatus! Trilogy* in return for the promise that I not tell anyone, lest he be charged with corrupting a minor. But at fourteen, I didn't know what to make of the book, so I mostly thumbed through the sex scenes and returned it to Larry a month later.

Reading *The Illuminatus! Trilogy* as an adult, as I did late last year, was a kind of revelation. The book—which is actually three smaller volumes mashed together into a single text—defies description. It was, according to authors Robert Shea and

Robert Anton Wilson, conceived in the late 1960s during their tenure as associate editors of *Playboy* magazine's Forum, a section devoted to reader correspondence on the subject of civil liberties. Shea and Wilson received a near-steady stream of "paranoid rantings from people imagining totally baroque conspiracies." At some point, the duo decided to write a novel that would consider what might happen if every possible conspiracy theory was not only real but also interconnected.

The resultant saga has been described by Wilson as an exercise in "guerilla ontology." It is nominally about a millennia-old conflict between the global Illuminati that secretly controls world governments, and the Discordian Society, an Eris-worshiping chaos religion. To Shea and Wilson's credit, both factions draw as much on historical reference as they do on surrealist fantasy. The true identities of the Illuminati are wrapped in a series of guises specific enough to evoke plausibility: the Freemasons, the Founding Fathers, the Nazis, the mafia, the CIA. Likewise the trilogy's Discordians are drawn from an actual pseudo-religion of the same name that was founded in the early 1960s as something halfway between a prank and an LSD-inflected riff on Zen Buddhism, and with which Wilson was loosely associated.

It's hard not to marvel at the way *The Illuminatus! Trilogy* savages the concept of believability. Despite its remarkable depth of research, the trilogy refuses to distinguish between the credible and the credulous. Over the course of its wanderings,

it presents a still-living John Dillinger (in hiding under an assumed identity), the lost continent of Atlantis, a talking dolphin, a battalion of hibernating Nazis, and a rakish proto-libertarian submarine captain named Hagbard Celine, who periodically makes reference to an Ayn Rand–satire text entitled "Telemachus Sneezed" while simultaneously expounding upon the value of free will and drug use. Moreover, *The Illuminatus! Trilogy* is written in a compositional style not unlike an exquisite corpse. Point of view, tenses, and even characters' identities shift midscene where Shea and Wilson have traded the manuscript back and forth, one-upping each other with ever more ridiculous scenarios.

If the style of *The Illuminatus! Trilogy* tends toward the aggressively postmodern, its underlying message is more straightforward. In knotting conspiracy and truth into a serpent with neither head nor tail, the book says more about the state of America in the late 1960s than it does about the secrets with which it claims to be concerned. Below its surface are clearer markers of implication—a pivotal scene set amid the 1968 Democratic convention riots; an obsessive returning to the JFK assassination; an implication of organized religion as fraudulent and hollow; a contemplation of uninhibited sex, psychedelic drugs, and their subversive power. It is, in its way, a remarkable record of the country's collective fears during a period of unprecedented social and political upheaval. When the Discordian Hagbard Celine is asked to describe the Illuminati's agenda, he offers a tellingly specific list: "Universal electronic surveillance. No-knock laws. Stop and frisk laws. Government inspection of first-class mail. Automatic fingerprinting, photographing, blood tests, and urinanalysis of any person arrested before he is charged with a crime. A law making it unlawful to resist even unlawful arrest." It is perhaps no surprise then that *The Illuminatus! Trilogy* makes more than a passing nod to Pynchon's *Gravity's Rainbow*, the other massive 1970s tome that attempted to wring similar metaphysical meaning from America's Vietnam-era cultural schizophrenia.

So it's strange to read *The Illuminatus! Trilogy* at a time when real people suspect Hillary Clinton of being a witch, and of running a child sex-trafficking ring out of a DC pizza restaurant. Alex Jones, incendiary founder of the alt-right darling Infowars, has previously accused the government of staging the Sandy Hook shooting with paid actors, and connected 9/11 to the JFK assassination, all at the behest of the very same global Illuminati parodied in the book. The polarity of our suspicion seems to have reversed, no longer a spiritual conflict between brave psychonauts and their FBI bogeymen, but more of an internet-powered search for scapegoats in an age of diminishing expectations. Around the world, progressive thought faces a dual assault from plutocrats for whom it is a financial inconvenience and nationalists for whom it is an easy villain. In May of this year, Jones was granted a White House press pass, while the angry white men who appear in the background of every Trump rally look increasingly like those long-ago tabletop war gamers from Men at Arms.

If the lunatics are now truly running the asylum, then Shea and Wilson have been warning us for a great many years not just of their potential rise, but of how effective their fantasies of persecution would prove to the ruling class. When every conspiracy is true, anyone is entitled to be a victim. There is little practical difference between cries of "fake news" and the possibility of a lost Nazi battalion hibernating beneath the fictitious Lake Totenkopf. Paranoia claims no political allegiance, only emotional expediency; if Obama is a secret Muslim, then so much the better to distract from the calamity of a lost job or a shuttered factory or a staggering medical bill. In the meantime, our leaders continue to bomb the Middle East with automated flying robots and monitor citizens through glossy thousand-dollar mobile phones, and *The Illuminatus! Trilogy* seems to understand this, even some forty years after its publication. As it turns out, the conspiracy that runs deepest is the one that we can all plainly see.

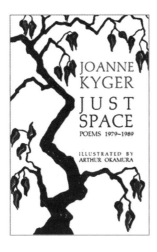

ON JOANNE KYGER'S
Just Space: Poems 1979-1989

CASSANDRA CLEGHORN

In the dog days of summer, when Vermont is at its greenest, I get homesick for California's extremes. I watch video clips of great white shark sightings off the Goleta Pier and fires consuming thousands of acres of chaparral a few miles from my childhood home. As the Santa Anas rage, I hear Joan Didion's voice: *The wind shows us how close to the edge we are*. I reach for those poets fed on drought and fog, whose work returns me to the place where I became the reader and writer I am: Brenda Hillman's *Cascadia*, or Eleni Sikélianòs's *The California Poem*, but also, and especially, everything by poet Joanne Kyger. Of Kyger's more than thirty books, *Just Space: Poems 1979-1989* is my favorite.

Kyger, who passed away in the spring of 2017 at the age of eighty-two, was a prolific and singular poet, if also relatively unknown outside her circles of adoring friends, students, and fellow writers. Kyger's writing is fresh, immediate, and undefensive—engaging with almost every modern American school or movement, and yet irreducible to any one. Published by many small presses, including City Lights in San Francisco, Two Windows Press in Berkeley, and Blue Press in Santa Cruz, Kyger had only two books of poems issued by nationally known houses: Dutton in 1983, and Penguin in 2002. A posthumous volume of previously unpublished work—*There You Are: Interviews, Journals, and Ephemera*, edited by Cedar Sigo, is just out from Wave Books.

The design of *Just Space* sets it apart from Kyger's other books. The cover of heavyweight, ridged, cream-colored paper features a dramatic ink drawing by the poet's Bolinas neighbor Arthur Okamura. Framed by branches and leaves, Kyger's name appears in large red font, Goudy Old Style. Thick lavender endpapers match a color in the cover. There are no blurbs. Such elegant details are the signature of Black Sparrow Press, the great publishing house founded by John and Barbara Martin in the 1960s that represented Paul Bowles, Robert Creeley, Denise Levertov, Kenneth Koch, Robert Duncan, Diane Wakoski, Michael McClure, Charles Bukowski, John Yau, and others. (In this regard, it makes perfect sense that Kyger's last work would be published by Wave, the contemporary press that most clearly recalls Black Sparrow in its commitment to the tight union of literary style, sensibility, and book design.)

Black Sparrow Press closed its doors fifteen years ago, its inventory and standing obligations to authors lovingly transferred to David Godine after a partial merger with Ecco. ("This wasn't an acquisition; this was a gift," Godine told *Poets and Writers* shortly after the transfer. "It was an act of unspeakable generosity.") As a young writer in Santa Barbara, where many of the Martins' books were produced, I was drawn to the brand. Holding *Just Space* now returns me to the Book Den on East Anapamu Street, where I found books organized not by author, but by press—Capra, New Directions, Black Sparrow. I read the spines like runes, choosing books that promised to teach me not only what makes a poem but also what draws writers into conversation with one another on the page.

Kyger's book is full of such conversations. Drinking tequila on the beach with friends, watching crows, splitting wood, trying to meditate, writing, writing, always writing, Kyger asks: "Is this the form / I come home to?" Her mix of insecurity and chutzpah ("Marked, bespattered & understood") is as much a part of the landscape as are the starlings and gulls, purple meadow grasses, "spumes of whales." In one poem, she describes going to a "big Poetry Reading" in San Francisco with McClure: "I am very very nervous," she writes. "I wonder if the car / will make it / I think I may die at any moment." In another poem, set at a "posh" artist's retreat, she refuses utensils and "the large damask napkin," demonstrating "how to eat / just with the hands."

She worries over the problem of what kind of poem to write: "You like it huh? You like that dulcet stuff? / Inside language school?" A few lines later, she asserts: "*I am the I* / of this writing which indeed I like to do." The cast of characters in this book numbers in the dozens. Well-known personalities (Bill Berkson, Ted Berrigan, Jack Spicer, Philip Whalen, Bobbie Louise Hawkins, et alia) hang out with friends tagged by first name only. But Kyger never loses herself in this crowd. The five-line poem called "Itsy Bitsy Polka Dot Review" gleams with Kyger's unmistakable voice:

Well, I'll never *sell* myself
out of whatever I've *got* which is,
    these days, folks
which is these days, folks
is, um
darn hard to come by.

The verve, formal looseness (what we now might call "hybridity"), and sheer presence of Kyger's poems speak to contemporary poetic practices and, perhaps surprisingly, social media. "How much time / can I spend / regaining these refreshing circumferences of the day," Kyger asks, as if in anticipation of our daily scrolling through archives of moments. Telephones and typewriters are Kyger's favorite ways to fill her "definite need to be reassured / that the present has always existed." Poet and critic Stephanie Burt has written recently about how the fragmentary style of new memoirs "seem[s] to fit our age of distraction and hyper-alertness, when we might look up from Proust, or from the Grand Canyon, to see if we've been retweeted, or liked, or tagged." Ditto Kyger, who did most of her writing generations before Twitter.

For all her social butterflying, there's also a steady dose of solitary presence in *Just Space*—an aloneness that is constantly infiltrated by the social, despite the poet's desire to withdraw. Snippets of conversation (in her head? on the line?) interrupt her attempts "to chronicle / events economically / and learn how to sit." With seeming offhandedness, Kyger combines countless shades of irony—exasperation, irreverence, and more—with her compassion for fellow precarious beings, human and nonhuman. "And so what's 'Buddhist' / about all this // landscape consciousness / and its fragile human frequency?" Kyger offers this sunny answer: "Company that's what / it's all about entwined / in the same air and waking / in the same sun's dawn." *Just Space* draws me into the bright world of Kyger's making.

ON HAMPTON HAWES'S

Raise Up Off Me

CHRIS CARROLL

Three years into a ten-year drug sentence, the jazz pianist Hampton Hawes watched on TV as JFK accepted the presidency. The next day, as he recounts in his memoir, *Raise Up Off Me*—one of the best and most tragically overlooked jazz memoirs ever written—he told a medical officer that he wanted to apply for a presidential pardon. The officer said, "That's the root of your trouble, Hampton, you refuse to be realistic. When you leave here you're probably going to go back to dope because you'll still be thinking unrealistic."

Hawes had been put away in 1958 by an undercover cop who had posed as a fan and gradually insinuated himself into Hawes's good graces, finally busting him on a heroin charge. Until then, Hawes, a heavy user, had been one of the most in-demand pianists on the scene—he played with Charlie Parker, Miles Davis, Charles Mingus, and Billie Holiday, among others, and was a leader in his own right, widely admired for his ability to play paradoxically unhurried, laid-back rhythms at bebop's breakneck tempos.

The form to apply for presidential pardon arrived over a year after Hawes first saw JFK on TV, and he immediately set about his work. "What I did was send John Kennedy a directive: as you are the Commander-in-Chief it is my duty as a citizen to inform you that an injustice has been perpetrated, one of your people is being subjected to cruel and unusual punishment, and it is your duty to consider the evidence and reciprocate . . . And then to round it off I added some heavy legal shit in Latin I'd dug up in the library."

He sent the form off early in 1963. Months passed. News trickled in from the outside: his friend, the pianist Sonny Clark, had OD'd in New York; his mother had a heart attack. One morning in August 1963, he woke up, "just as I'd been doing for five years, took my little funny case into the can to wash up and brush my teeth, headed for chow as usual, here's another day, man, and was stopped by a security guard." The guard escorted him to the head of the psychiatric ward, who gave him the news: "Executive clemency granted by authority of the President of the United States."

This is among the most moving scenes in a memoir that is by turns funny, frank, and deeply sad. Hawes is a wonderful narrator with an instinctive ability to tell a story. He describes cruising down Manhattan's Seventh Avenue with Thelonious Monk and Nica Rothschild (the famous jazz baroness) in her Bentley, with "Miles pulling alongside in his Mercedes, calling through the window in his little hoarse voice cut down by a throat operation, 'Want to race?' Nica nodding, then turning to tell us in her prim British tones: 'This time I believe I'm going to beat the motherfucker.'"

The book is also unerringly insightful about what the music meant to the men playing it. Writing in retrospect from the 1970s, Hawes remembers, "Though we were rebelling, we were doing it musically, nonviolently, and most people didn't know what was coming down. Now there's another generation of rebels and these kids are doing things we wouldn't have dared because we knew we wouldn't have got away with it and were smart enough not to try."

In fact, it's not quite right to say that Hawes wrote the memoir. It's more an as-told-to, something he produced with another piano player, Don Asher. The two met one night in the late '60s, when Hawes was several years out of prison, and rock had long since eclipsed jazz, forcing Hawes to take a gig in a down-and-out bar. Asher came in one night, recognized Hawes, and they got to talking, eventually agreeing to work together on Hawes's memoir. Asher labored to capture Hawes's voice, the cadences of his speech, and his virtuosic ability to curse, helping to write, in the end, a book that sounds remarkably fresh some fifty-odd years later.

I would never have known about Hawes's book if it weren't for Asher, who also wrote under his own name. Years after Asher died, Lewis Lapham, the longtime editor of *Harper's* who had discovered him and published his writing in the 1970s, pointed me toward Asher's work. Much of it was collected and published in *Notes from a Battered Grand, A Memoir: Fifty Years of Music, from Honky-Tonk to High Society*, now sadly out of print.

One of the things I've found so fascinating about these books is the way each man's story seems an inversion of the other's—Hawes's an account of a preternatural talent who played at the highest levels of the instrument with some of the greatest musicians ever known; Asher's the story of a man who, though no slouch himself, spent most of his life playing roadside dives, strip clubs, and cocktail lounges, and touring with third-rate big bands that played remote towns and insurance conventions.

Where Hawes's book is full of intimate portraits of giants like Charlie Parker and Billie Holiday, Asher's captures the quotidian humor of the gigging musicians who never made it into the spotlight. "In Rome, New York," he writes of one of his big band tours, "the band was interviewed by a radio disk jockey, who asked, during a discussion of creative expression, what images went through our minds while we were improvising. Nelly answered truthfully that he might be wondering how the jar of mayonnaise in his bag was holding up during the current hot spell, or if the bag of cabbage and lettuce he'd left on a motel window sill in Schenectady had wilted by now. The d.j. thought Nelly was

jiving him, laughed abruptly, glared, and went on to the next player."

With each new gig, Asher, wry and funny, gives the impression of Odysseus washing up on the shore of a foreign land, not knowing what to expect, though in this case the flesh-eating cannibals are replaced by roomfuls of fat, dancing salesmen funneling booze and demanding polkas.

The books overlap in wonderful ways, each touching on the difficulties faced by jazz musicians when rock arrived. Where Asher seems to lament a lost sensibility—what he calls "Cole Porter's champagne sophistication"—Hawes sees more an opportunity, and the great pleasure of his later music (in spite of critical dismissal) is the way in which he continues to grow and change, adapting to rock's innovations. And they both discuss the essential question of what it means to swing, and how someone can really learn to play jazz, a question that Asher raises repeatedly and that Hawes takes up and answers:

> A critic once wrote that I was "the key figure in the current crisis surrounding the funky school of jazz piano." Shit, there wasn't no crisis. All he meant was that I can get down and I can swing. And if he could have looked deep into my life he would have learned that the reason I play the way I do is that I'm taking the years of being … denied love and holding in my natural instincts when I was a kid, of listening to the beautiful spirituals in my father's church and going

in the back doors of clubs to play for white audiences, of getting strung and burned in the streets and locked up in dungeons when I tried to find my way—taking all that natural bitterness and suppressed animal feeling out on the piano. That's why I can swing. There really ain't no secret.

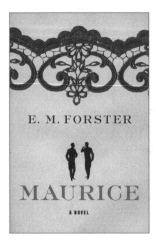

ON E. M. FORSTER'S

Maurice

JOSEPH FRANKEL

I first read *Maurice* after my favorite professor mentioned that E. M. Forster was gay. She said that Forster had written a novel about two men in love and kept it hidden until his death. It was never assigned to me in school. Instead, we read the much more famous *A Room with a View*, which is peak Forster: a wealthy young woman in a "muddle" about who she is and what she wants is on the verge of walling herself into a conventional life, until, at the last minute, she runs away with the thoughtful, handsome stranger she meets in Italy.

Squint just a little and the plot of *Maurice* looks similar. The novel, written in 1913 and 1914 and then revised several times, follows an upper-class British boy named Maurice (pronounced Morris) who recognizes from an early age that he is attracted to men. At Cambridge, he falls in love with a fellow student named Clive Durham, who eventually leaves him for a woman. Maurice, miserable, tries to curb his desire—even stomp it out with the help of a hypnotist—but ultimately runs away with Clive's gamekeeper, Alec Scudder.

From childhood, Maurice conforms and chameleons, preparing to step into a life that England has cut out for him. The narrator belabors the point that—outward appearances aside—Maurice is extremely repressed. From the book's beginning, he has a cryptic, recurring dream in which a voice presents him with a "friend." The dream itself is vague, but Forster makes it abundantly clear this is an allusion to male-male love. (Maurice, meanwhile, imagines the voice refers to Jesus, or perhaps a Greek god, concluding "most probably he was just a man.") This vision echoes in the waking world throughout the rest of the book. The dream also feels like a fitting device in a book about repressed desire. Dreams, like fiction, can be chimeric: part picture of reality as it is, part as the dreamer wants it to be.

Maurice suggests why Forster would so invest himself in the story of a stifled, confused, wealthy, presumably straight young woman. Her story is his with a difference: he could give his heroine a happy ending. Forster wanted the same for Maurice. He wrote that "a happy ending was imperative" for *Maurice*: "I was determined that in fiction anyway two men should fall in love and remain in it for the ever and ever that fiction allows . . . I dedicated it 'To a Happier Year' and not altogether vainly."

However, had Forster published his book in which two men are happily in love, he would have faced scandal at least and persecution at the hands of law at worst.

As a writer, Forster has been criticized for a quality of boredom in his books. Like Forster's other works, *Maurice* contains digressions about the intricacies of Cambridge and country homes, and Victorian abstractions about Life and Love that might alienate or fall flat. Of *Maurice*, it's been written that Scudder feels shoehorned in as a convenient deus ex machina who literally comes to Maurice's window while Maurice shouts out in his sleep. (Forster later acknowledged that the Scudder chapters were add-ons.) Much of the book feels as if it was difficult for Forster in two senses: difficult for him to imagine this kind of relationship being possible and difficult for him to write and put his name to.

I know the feeling, in fiction and elsewhere, of casting out a line, hoping to draw out a coherent account of a mind, a body, a self, a life, and to come up with only broken pieces or a caricature. And yet if we were only to speak in moments of perfect coherence, of perfect confidence, the world would be near silent.

I won't say *Maurice* changed my life. I did not come to it—as I have with other books, as I imagine most people who read fiction have—at a time that felt too lucky to be coincidence. What I did get from *Maurice* was a stark reminder that silence, at least in my case, is a choice. That I could choose to reject it with far greater ease than someone who had to consider if the book he was writing would land him in jail.

But still I am tempted to follow Forster's lead. Especially casting my mind further back in history to Forster's time, in which writing even this column might have ruined my life, or instead into the worst version of the future, in which the result would be the same.

All this to say I still think about this book not because of its merits but because it feels familiar. Unlike *A Room with a View*, *Howards End*, or *A Passage to India*, through *Maurice* I know, or have the illusion that I know, Forster. My own hesitation to write about my personal life, my queerness, in published work allows me to sympathize. It educates my guess as to why, even in the late '60s, Forster kept his book unpublished. Shame runs deep. It is quiet. It eludes language and is immune to the reason to which language can give voice.

For all its flaws, *Maurice* does something remarkable: it envisions a happy ending for two men in love at a time when that seemed impossible.

Over one hundred years later, even in the absence of strict censorship laws in the UK and the US, a queer story with a happy ending is no small or usual thing. From *Buffy the Vampire Slayer* to *The Amazing Adventures of Kavalier & Clay*, so many pages and screens are littered with the broken bodies and minds of queer people who come to harm by way of punishment or ridiculous coincidence.

A lot of fiction with queer characters, such as *Giovanni's Room* and "Brokeback Mountain"—the list goes on and on—has the defense of verisimilitude: it draws from the tragic source material of real life. The news often brings bleak stories about discrimination and the violation of civil rights throughout the world: the Pulse nightclub shooting, the state-sanctioned violence against queer people in Chechnya and beyond, the litany of hate crimes reported on in the US. All of this may understandably lead queer people to fear, to find it difficult to imagine anything but tragedy, even in fictional circumstances. Which is why we need fiction that documents the realities of loneliness and violence of the time and place it represents but that can also go beyond these realities. Great queer art walks this line.

Forster didn't think a more permissive future would come to pass. In the book's postscript, written in 1960, he predicts that the Wolfenden report, a government-sponsored study that argued for legalized homosexuality, will be "indefinitely rejected." But for the most part, Forster was wrong. He failed to imagine what would soon be possible. The Sexual Offences Act 1967—several years after Forster's bleak prediction—legalized consensual sex between men above the age of twenty-one. (Laws regulating homosexuality in England never acknowledged same-sex relationships between women.) Despite the change, Forster still kept the book from publication until his death, three years later.

Whatever his reasons, Forster had both the audacity to envision safety and joy for a queer couple at a time when they were available to so few and the awareness to realize how few got close to it. It might be hard for contemporary readers and writers to understand how great a feat that was in 1913.

The filmmakers James Ivory and Ismail Merchant—themselves a couple—did. That's why they fought to make *Maurice* into a movie at the height of the HIV/AIDS crisis, even though they weren't crazy about the source material, and the keepers of Forster's estate were reluctant to have *Maurice* on the screen (they felt the book was weak). After the film—which has strengths the book lacks—was made, Ivory claims that people came up to him on the street and thanked him for making it. As men like Maurice—and many people unlike him—were dying in droves, the film offered comfort and hope at a time when seeing two men together on-screen, and alive, was rare.

Today, when hateful beliefs are growing in boldness and visibility, there is daily proof that there is no easy, linear progress. Acceptance and safety are not guaranteed. In such a time it feels worthwhile to remember a piece of art that, despite an inhospitable world, kept alive the possibility of "a happier year."

ON DAPHNE MARLATT'S

Ana Historic

ROHAN MAITZEN

There's a spectacular view from the twelfth floor of Buchanan Tower, where the University of British Columbia's Department of History is housed. Deep evergreen forests encircle the campus; beyond them the steel-blue waters of Burrard Inlet cross to the North Shore Mountains, providing a majestic backdrop for the city of Vancouver. Through the west-facing windows of the study room where I once had a carrel, the sunsets are so extravagantly beautiful that it could be difficult to concentrate on my work. The perspective within the department, though, was often less inspiring. "You're trying to change something in your culture!" expostulated one fellow student, angrily pushing his chair back from the seminar table as we argued over including feminist readings on a course syllabus.

I also sometimes studied in a stuffy room on the fourth floor. This one had no windows at all, but the welcoming atmosphere made up for the lack of panoramic vistas. It was the domain of the Department of English, and I shared this space because I had badgered the bureaucrats into letting me be the first UBC student to pursue an honors degree in both English and history. It was the late 1980s and interdisciplinarity was no more in vogue on campus than feminism: the only common ground in my dual program was me. As I shuttled back and forth between floors, though, I found myself also crossing and recrossing intellectual boundaries that seemed increasingly artificial—and increasingly gendered. Isn't history, after all, just a specific kind of storytelling? Don't novelists often tell true stories about the past? And doesn't enforcing the line between history and fiction end up particularly limiting the stories we can tell about women's lives?

Books have an uncanny way of appearing in your life exactly when you need them most. With nice serendipity, Daphne Marlatt's novel *Ana Historic* was published just as I was struggling to articulate answers to these questions. Fragmented, exploratory, provocative, *Ana Historic* proposes new stories and new forms, reaching beyond the conventional limits of both history and fiction. Annie, the novel's narrator, is a former graduate student who abandoned her own history degree to marry Richard, one of her professors. Annie has let her identity be subsumed in her husband's, accepting his boilerplate acknowledgement as

compensation: "to my wife without whose patient assistance this book would never have been completed." This, her anxious mother raised her to believe, is "a woman's place. safe. suspended out of the swift race of the world." Now, however, Annie recoils at "the monstrous lie of it: the lure of absence, self-effacing." Waking in the night as Richard snores comfortably beside her, she feels lost, adrift: "the story has abandoned me."

But what if there were another story? Gradually, Annie awakens to different, liberating possibilities. The process begins when, while doing Richard's research in the Vancouver city archives, she comes across a rare passing reference to a woman in the man's world of what was then a rough frontier town:

'The first piano on the south side of
Burrard Inlet was one which was . . .
sold to Mrs. Richards, school teacher,
who lived in a little three-room cottage
back of the Hastings Mill schoolhouse,
and afterwards married Ben Springer.'

"There is a story here," Annie thinks, but "that is all that history says": "she buys a piano and afterwards marries Ben Springer, as if they were cause and effect." History, as Richard likes to remind her, "is built on a groundwork of fact," but to tell Mrs. Richards's story, Annie needs something else: "i don't want history's voice. i want . . ."

What she wants, it turns out, is *Ana Historic* itself. In her hybrid text, Marlatt interleaves fragments of different elements—archival excerpts, Annie's auto-biographical reflections, Mrs. Richards's experience—giving no more authority to what is known than to what is imagined or desired. Into this undisciplined space, Mrs. Richards emerges, rechristened Ana ("back, backward, reversed / again, anew"), "free to look out at the world with her own eyes, free to create her vision of it."

Annie begins by reconstructing Ana's life, filling in the gaps, turning her absence into presence. This reclamation of narrative space is the familiar work of historical fiction, and of much women's history. As Ana's story approaches Ben Springer's accepted proposal, however, Annie chafes against following the facts along "that path that led to marriage or death, no other fork in the trail":

> what if that life should close in on
> her like the lid of a hope chest? if she
> should shrivel and die inside, con-
> stricted by the narrow range of what
> was acceptable for Mrs. Springer? if
> all the other selves she might be were
> erased?

"That fiction, that lie that you can't change the ending!": "the truth is," Annie reflects, thinking of her conventional mother, and of her own safe, conventional choices, "our stories are hidden from us by fear"—what might we find, where might we go, if we could overcome it?

> the silence of trees
> the silence of women

> if they could speak
> an unconditioned language
> what would they say?

For Ana, the answer comes with "a sudden rush of desire" that Annie herself can barely keep up with: "you've taken the leap into this new possibility and i can't imagine what you would say." Then as Annie finally escapes her fear, she finds her way to a happy ending for herself as well—Zoe:

> she asks me to present myself, to take
> the leap, as the blood rushes into my
> face and i can speak: you. i want you.
> *and me.* together.

Ultimately history and fiction both fall away, leaving Annie with poetry:

> it isn't dark but the luxury of being
> has woken you, the reach of your
> desire, reading
> us into the page ahead.

It's an exhilarating and somewhat vertiginous conclusion, one I have been thinking about and also arguing with for decades now. My own instincts are more prosaic; I am pulled up more often by the warning Annie hears but transcends:

> come back, history calls, to the solid
> ground of fact. you don't want to fall
> off the edge of the world—

Rereading it now, *Ana Historic* seems a little dated, too, with its invocation of *écriture féminine*, its appeal to writing through the body, its self-conscious lowercase "i." Its metafiction is less novel now, its feminism less subversive—though these are signs, I hope, that we have indeed, at least a little bit, changed something in our culture. In its own way, *Ana Historic* is now a historical document. But rereading it also reminds me of the excitement I felt discovering the kind of woman, writer, and scholar I would be, and of the debt I owe to writers like Marlatt, who pushed past the boundaries I too contested. As Zoe tells Annie, "it's women imagining all that women could be that brings us into the world."

NOCTURNE

What was rampant in me was not wysteria. Perhaps decay, or loss of reflection.

No one like me gets old, or so I thought, even as I watched the days fade into each other.

Was I no one? Which phrase means a grown-up girl: mica-gilded; pure myth; gone?

Thoreau might say I was trying to find the door to nothingness, that the wild was
   already in me.

However, I walked out of my bed to find my skin, only to return moondrunk, bramble-
   laden, stripped

to sinew, a broken syntax. No denying how I got here, I lay down among the tall grass

and came up a specter. I came up everywhere.

RIGOROUS PRACTICE OF LISTENING

By which I mean we let the day pass between us
without either of us saying *go on* or *stay*, saying much of anything.
That when you did speak it was in the language of birds—your hands raised
as wings to your mouth blowing in and out
the birds came from their high places amongst the pines,
singing back to you.

There was the man whom you said nothing to but kissed his forehead
after he'd caught us three fish. And the man who fixed your cars
who never spoke. The stranger you shared a cigar with in front of the grocery store.
The way you held the package of red beans from your brother back home. I heard it all.

Who knows how your brilliant uncles died,
or how many people you saw given over to trees
or left on the train tracks.
When I ask you about fear, you take me to the nectarine tree
where the Japanese beetles have eaten halfway through
"I can't kill them," you say, "but they'll destroy the whole yard."

Communications

Sofi Stambo

W e work on the fifth floor Communications Department. It's a typical office: very little space, a lot of people sitting on top of each other. We shoot emails, execute reports and kill invoices. It's a war zone so it's very important to exchange pleasantries while talking behind each other's backs. You need to be able to produce a pleasantry at any given moment. I learned from the best, Patty, the owner's assistant, who always smiles and compliments my shoes, shirt, hair, bag, rings, panties, bra. She always finds something which she likes about your immediate presence. If you're really hard to like, she'll compliment you on the fax you just received. She never fails, can't afford to, her salary depends on that. It's amazing how good it makes you feel when she says I like your (fill in the blank) even though you know that she doesn't.

Compliments go really well with pats on the back, which I like too. So at around a quarter to ten, after you do your rounds with compliments and back-patting, you need a piece of office gossip. Then you can say you have a life because people look forward to seeing you and talking to you. You are somebody.

But I always had troubles with the portion of the job involving the supply and demand of gossip. So after the fifth person stalked me at the fax machine to ask me how the new woman was, I decided to actually pay more attention to her.

She lives alone, this new Cindy person. Alone here means not married, no kids, no pets. Turns out I didn't have to work hard to learn that much about her. This is because she talks a lot, the way lonely people do. Also she doesn't really listen when you respond. And she confessed that she spent the entire weekend looking for mice eggs in her apartment. The first thing I think is, if she had a husband or a child one of them would have explained to her the evolution of species, mice in particular and how they have wombs in which they carry children pretty much the same way we do. I also think if she had a dog or a cat, she wouldn't be looking for mice, period. See what I'm saying? Let alone their eggs.

What else about Cindy, I've heard her coughing laughter, which is an unmistakable sign of flirtation, heterosexual in her case. She did that very early in the game, to the two good-looking men in our company. What that showed me was average taste and sexual starvation, combined with inexperience and vulnerability.

If you are a worldly woman, like I am, you'd use sexual cough sparingly around here. You'd notice that one of your objects of affection, Paul, is married and probably loves his wife since he constantly inserts her into his sentences and also her photo frames all over his desk. You would notice too that the second one, Peter, has issues larger than any of us can comprehend, and is twenty to thirty years younger than you.

I always had troubles with the portion of the job involving the supply and demand of gossip.

So the first big storm erupted on day four. Peter (with the problems) approached Cindy's desk and she automatically started talking as if she was sucking on a candy, licking a lollipop, and chewing gum at the same time. She overused her tongue, twisting and smacking it against her cheeks and licking her lips. The woman was being sexy the best way she knew how. He wanted her to send a fax but she said that it would have to wait until Friday. This is the kind of delay that is meant to say "I am unattainable," a foreplay type of thing, like, "I am not always available for you." What she didn't see was that, first of all, Peter didn't want her love and affection. And second of all, he wanted things done immediately. Because that would make him look good in front of the boss, who also happens to be his uncle. Third, Peter has zero interest in older women. Fourth, he has anger management problems not as big as hers, but big enough.

What happened next was that Peter got really red and started screaming at her. He told her that he could fire her sorry ass if he wanted to, since this is his great-uncle's company and she is desecrating the family by refusing to fax when there is a need to fax. He used that word "desecrating." I could see her go through all the reactions. She was first surprised to realize that her sex appeal wasn't working. Then, she was angry that she had wasted it on someone so simultaneously cold and red. She started to explain that her ass was anything but sorry after all this gym and tennis. And finally she lost it.

As I say that, I'm already freaking out because if she's able to tune in to my microwaves or whatever they call them and hear that I'm not only quietly monitoring the situation but also preparing to loudly discuss her in the fax machine area or in front of the women's bathroom, then I can see her losing it on me the way she did on Peter.

She glared at Peter over her glasses with her round eyes, which became even rounder when she is mad. She usually wears these small glasses, I don't know why, since she never uses them for looking through, you know, directly. I guess she bought them so she could look down on people and things. The glasses are always on the edge of her nose and then come her eyes and on top of that, her bangs with the highlights, and that's your classic Cindy right there.

She came very close to Peter, and I thought for a second that she was either going to kiss him or bite his nose off. Then she lowered her voice two octaves below his. And she started spitting all sorts of moral concepts at him, which boiled down to, essentially, "Who do you think you are to talk to ME! I am a grown woman." Here she introduced the theme of grown people, who are old enough and had taken enough bullshit in their lives to have the right to scream, "Enough is enough!" and throw a few things. She tried to throw the fax, but the sound it made was too quiet and it didn't so much fly as fall down. She grabbed two framed pictures of Paul's wife and threw them down, finally making enough noise to prove her point. And she had a valid point, just not very original.

She followed that with something along the lines of "I've never seen such an office in my whole life understand her life has been long—and I don't know how you people get anything done here. Where I come from . . ." It was never clear exactly where she came from, or why she left, but it is somewhere big and important and mentioned only to make us feel small and insignificant. We immediately did, we practice that often and are good at it.

She got distracted for a while and took a commercial break to talk about her ex-boss at her old job. Without changing her angry voice, she yelled a story at us about the boss snorting cocaine until his nose bled, so there were all these bloody Kleenexes on his desk, which no one wanted to pick up. She never finishes that story, and got distracted once again. I am guessing she picked up the Kleenexes herself, or didn't, but in both cases I do know she didn't let anybody walk all over her. At the end she repeated the word "harassment" a few times and that did it. Peter ran away.

The annoying thing is that I've got the feeling I don't have a solid piece of gossip for the fax machine area. On one hand I can just not go there ever again. But on the other hand, there are all these faxes to fax, and the last thing I want to do is desecrate the family.

As I listen to Cindy, I know that my eyes are also getting rounder and I nod a lot. My daughter told me that recently I've started to nod like crazy. I don't know if that is Cindy-related or if it's because I am also a grown woman and I've become wiser and better able to understand the human condition. Or maybe I only understand Cindy, with her angry, lonely, highlighted soul.

I pet her on the back and compliment her on her glasses. I ask her to please be a dear and send a few faxes for me at the fax machine area. I tell her that I am personally amazed how her faxes always go through. 🔖

AFTER ALL

"After all," that too might be possible . . .
—JOHN ASHBERY

It isn't too late, but for what I'm not sure.
Though I live for possibility, I loathe unbridled
Speculation, let alone those vague attempts
At self-exploration that become days wasted
Trying out the various modes of being:
The ecstatic mode, which celebrates the world, a high
That fades into an old idea; the contemplative,
Which says, *So what?* and leaves it there;
The skeptical, a way of being in the world
Without accepting it (whatever that might mean).
They're all poses, adequate to different ends
And certain ages, none of them conclusive
Or sufficient to the day. I find myself surprised
By my indifference to what happens next:
You'd think that after almost seventy years of waiting
For the figure in the carpet to emerge I'd feel a sense of
Urgency about the future, rather than dismissing it
As another pretext for more idle speculation.
I'm happy, but I have a pessimistic cast of mind.
I like to generalize, but realize it's pointless,
Since everything is there to see. I love remembering

For its own sake and the feel of passing time
It generates, which lends it meaning and endows it
With a private sense of purpose—as though every life
Were a long effort to salvage something of its past,
An effort bound to fail in the long run, though it comes
With a self-defeating guarantee: the evaporating
Air of recognition that lingers around a name
Or rises from a page from time to time; or the nothing
Waiting at the end of age; whichever comes last.

COGITO REDUX

I know I'm a creation of my brain,
But once that genie escapes its bottle,
It gets to say what's real. *I'm* real,
It says, along with my brain, as the much
Maligned Descartes maintained, and he was right.
Any knowledge we might attain is due to *us*,
The plural of *me*, but I can't claim credit:
It's just that otherwise there'd be nobody there
To figure it out, nobody there to *know*.
It starts out with how things look
To *someone*, and goes on from there
To a tentative conclusion that's consistent
With whatever it explains, with how things *seem*,
With how they seem to me. Appearances
Are perspectival: nothing looks like anything
To no one, which is to say the view from nowhere
Isn't a view at all. We're empiricists in the broad sense
After all, trying to make sense of our experiences
Within the bounds of reason, and if reason leads to nobody,
It's empty. I may be an intuition, but I'm hardly blind:
The things I feel and see are all I have to go on,
And the stories I tell, however fragile,
Force themselves on me as true, as one by one

My friends keep dying. I haven't heard that sentence yet,
But it's a matter of time (everything's a matter of time)
Before my own image starts dissolving. For now
It still glares up at me, like the celebrated frog
At the bottom of the mug from which I drink to celebrate
This proof of my self, unable to stop believing in it
Even as, with studied curiosity, I await its dissolution.

SELFIE STICK

To snap yourself from half a life away,
With the City of Lights floating in the background
And a smile frozen on the same face you wore on a day
In 1985 in the garden of Hôtel des Marronniers,
The hotel we're staying in now. *On a day*:
What used to be a real time and an actual place
Isn't real anymore, although the person that I'd been
Is still real, and the eternal present I inhabit remains real too,
At least for now. What holds it together is internal to it,
Like the music of the mirror that arises out of nowhere
And continues forever, through the vagaries of adolescence
And middle age and the fear of gradually getting old,
Until it ends abruptly, for no reason, on a random afternoon,
The way a Patricia Highsmith character might die, in a freak fall
On a nondescript street thousands of miles from home.

It didn't happen. But something like it will in time,
And then time ends. Life seems necessary from the inside,
But from the outside it's contingent and terrifying,
With the precariousness of existence written on its face.
I keep waiting for the thing to happen, meanwhile
Holding it at arm's length, keeping it at bay.

MARSYAS

We think Marsyas is the only one
who changed, stepping forth
from the forest to challenge Apollo, staring at the god

he could never rival as if
into a harshly lit mirror, each recoiling

at what he found there: the jealousy knifed
inside the mortal talent, the cold perfection
threaded through with rage.

But then the muses stirred behind them.
And Marsyas, out the painful human wish
to be admired, cannot help but play.

And afterwards, the cutting,
the stripped corpuscles, the ruined mouth—

    Only after his victory would Apollo reach out
and clip three small muscles from the satyr's throat
and shoulders, and dry them on a rock, and string them between
the curved horns of his lyre. Then the god

would pull a song
through that tender sinew, telling himself

it was not the crying of one
who's lost everything he loves but the god's
own singing that he heard, and after which
the muses strained, because it was the song

of someone who knew what it was like
to be alive, which the god could not bear
to know, or to stop playing.

And so Apollo, unthinking, binds himself
to Marsyas: the god taking from his rival

fear and desire, the satyr hardened by the god's
cruel skill, until both songs

writhe inside each other, sung
by one who cannot understand death, and so

never understands what he plays,
knowing only how his hand
trembles over the plucked muscle:

adding, he thinks, something lower to the notes,
something sweeter, and infinitely strange.

PASIPHAË

So after M died, she turned
to the dog. His copper eyes, the sinewy
haunch muscles. The way he perched
by the door of M's study as if
sensing the body he missed
behind it. Something she would not
let herself feel, dry-eyed
at the funeral, refusing to gather
up the pants that still hung in his closet
M's last particles until,
out of some extravagant kindness
or perhaps pity, she gave the dog
his sweater. She watched
as the dog circled and pawed at it, tearing
up the tissuey material in his attempts
to fall asleep. *Impossible*
not to love such need, she thought, telling herself
it was this passion to come as close
as possible to what he'd never possess
that attracted her now: she could not stop
touching him, pulling him
to her, gathering the thick folds
of neck skin between her fingers, kneading
into her palms the hot, popcorn smell
of his ears, his feet. Waking

in bed to a misty smear spread
on her sheets, red welts on her chest
from where he scratched and bit her.
She wanted to make the dog feel
for her some part of what was powerful
about his grief for M. She even began
to hate M's things, the cashmere sweater
now tossed in the trash, books and pants
burned, pictures of him swept
off the bedroom shelf. *Grief,*
her mother said, when she came to visit,
excusing her daughter's furious
disposals. *Though be careful you don't
lose control of yourself,* she warned,
as if too much feeling must be
a diminishment. It was the same lecture
she'd been given in high school
the night a boy came hours
late for a date, and still she ran,
uncomplainingly, to meet him. *Aren't you
ashamed,* her mother had said
upon her return, meaning
how willingly she had let herself
be debased. But love was a debasement.
In their first few months of courtship, M

had liked to crawl at her feet
during sex, eating the crackers
she held out as communion wafers, dressed
in the priest's black chasuble
he'd found for them: some nightmare-
colored sheath he'd scared up
from a local drama theater's closet.
And she'd indulged him: their marriage,
their sex, she couldn't help it,
even when he asked her
to beat him, she did it: she'd never seen
anyone want something so nakedly before.

Three months after M's death, the dog
got fleas. And she watched him, mesmerized,
scratch at the thin skin of his ears, biting
at his legs and belly until they bled,
until she too let herself become
infested with them: her clothes, her sheets
speckled with the fat black pinheads
feasting on them both, the blood they shared
raising welts on her cheeks. *One body*,
M once said as they lay, tangled
together, her legs pressed between his—
or was it his between hers?—their long limbs
muscular and bare, covered in the late
afternoon light with the same

fine gold furze of hair. How close she'd come
to really loving him. *You must get rid*
of that animal, her mother declared
one night at the kitchen table, horrified
by her necklace of bites, her wolfish
eating habits. How greedily
she ate: the sad result, her mother thought,
of living too long alone. *You're little*
better than that dog, her mother
told her, at which point she rose
from the table, tossed her food to the floor,
and got down on all fours to eat it.

from ANGEL CITY WEST

Photos by
Mark Steinmetz

It seems true of all great art that the work is accompanied—and enchanted, even aurified—by a mythology of its making (or maker). In the case of Mark Steinmetz's *Angel City West*, the mythology revolves around the Zeus of American street photography, Garry Winogrand.

In 1983, when he was twenty-one years old, Steinmetz dropped out of the graduate program at Yale, and headed to Los Angeles. He wanted to broaden his vision of America, and he'd heard Winogrand was out there. In times bygone, their meeting could've been ascribed to fate. Story goes that Steinmetz drove Winogrand around LA so he could shoot whatever inspired him (and Winogrand's work from the time suggests literally *everything* did) from the passenger side window of his Fiat.

When we talk about influence, we're often searching for an accounting of where the work that moves us came from. This story about Winogrand is of interest only because of the tremendous photographer Steinmetz became. It teases our imagination, allows us to nourish the illusion that something more was taking place in that little Fiat, some wordless spiritual exchange, a kind of osmotic transfer of sensitivities or vision or, I don't know, élan.

But if there is anything of Winogrand living in *Angel City West*, it's small and homunculus-like, because these pictures show all the hallmarks of Steinmetz's later, mature work—they're imbued with the same dreamy listlessness and subtle humor, and are composed with the same evocative grace. What they show, more than anything, is a fledgling master coming into his own.

—*Cheston Knapp*

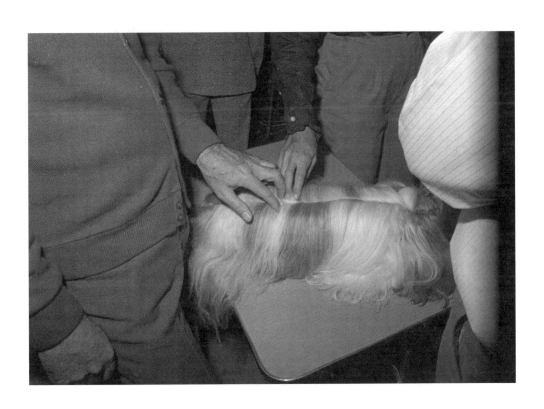

WAYS TO DRESS A FISH

No one expected a flood
despite sea displacing
sea despite old waters
waking

While the waters walked
                they talked

they kept their eyes on fire
but fire stayed put

They grew accustomed to the smoke
even liked the new sky—

    the way it coated their skin and mixed with beads of sweat

    the way it hid the whites of their eyes

    the way it settled on their tongues
the few remaining soft parts
down their throats

until they felt thick
and heavy

and full
           with their own soot

QAWANGUAQ WITH HOUSE

There was a house I needed
to go

I needed a home
   to survive
        to wait the fire
the flood where there were others
            with other
bodies

There was earth in them
           I dug
speaking
the dead   with words

I dug my way back
      to survive the flood
into the earth

I had to know what I didn't know
    I didn't know
what kind of monster was I

                       You can't throw a fish back in the water
                                 and expect it to swim—

So I dug.

I dug out a rib
and another's rib
     another

I dug deeper
    until

I reached the bottom of this

house I reached the cellar
where the center was cold

where I could hide

My body was full of bodies.

QAWANGUAQ

She coughed and the women came out
    violently
She opened her mouth and coughed out
    a small bird
She coughed out matted fur
        and fish with faces
        and the rocks
        she had tried to eat
    until
there was nothing left inside her
            but water   and red

She coughed out the water
and the sea rushed to fill
the thirsting places

She took back fire
      black fire-rock
and wrapped her many-body
in mountain
      still and moving
      many and
        one

She wrapped her body in mountain
and dug her feet beneath the water

                                        she spilled
where soft
                she could feel a hardness moving
                                  outward

She could feel many hearts
                        hard hearts
each small disturbance
                        press
the small rooms of her chest

Each sound in her chest
a heart
       a rock
dislodging   soft in the water

         until

           She was no body

AFTER

1.

We came to the island. We stayed in the house.
Rain and sun. Bougainvillea. Pink cedar.
How many shadows slipped along walls
or whetted the leaves of century plants?

2.

We saw clouds from the windows. Far boats.
You left the bed and came back shaking.
Your mother, her white hair, or something
whose shape would never, at last, find you.

3.

Night palms clattering like hungry bowls.
Crazy whistling of the island peepers.
We walked to the water. Walked back.
We walked to the water . . . walked back.

ELEGY, IN WORDS

And then everything unfastened—. Did the wind.
    Was it wind. Was it in the pines, or the window.
Were they beyond where they were before. Where
    was that. Barn owl, I know. Like a whisper, only
lower; whimper, louder. Nothing hurt, but something
    beckoning, and very near. You won't believe this.
Nothing like *who cooks for you* of the barred owl.

He was humming. So the coyote, calling back,
    her whelps yipping back, and the wood-pipe calling
of the close bird kept on—is that how you can tell.
    I would have slept through. I can't imagine,
they would maybe be fifty yards off, the rock ridge
    running beyond the pines. Not church, not
birthdays. He never sang, not one note.

I'd been there all day for days, like that, and humming.
    He played a finger game—squeezing. I know.
I gave him a touch of bourbon to his lips, with a straw,
    what a face. He wanted—. No, I burned him.
I can't tell you how long, but they kept calling
    each other in the pines. And then the phone.
That's the last he said to me in words. I can't imagine.

Elizabeth Bradfield

LESSON VIII: MAP OF NORTH AMERICA
—redacted from Smith's Quarto, or Second Book in Geography, *1848, p. 17*

division

division

        general divisions

      opposite

cluster   clusters   What considerable number

Where is

        Where is Cape Farewell?

What sound leads into   the largest

   What What What What

Boundaries   Bound United   Bound
   the   New ?   Bound   possessions?

   What What What What

prevails

   What What What What

races What   race   ?

A POEM AS LONG AS CALIFORNIA

This is my pastoral: that used-car lot
where someone read *Song of Myself* over the loudspeaker

all afternoon, to customers who walked among the cars
mostly absent to what they heard,

except for the one or two who looked up
into the air, as though they recognized the reckless phrases

hovering there with the colored streamers,
their faces suddenly loose with a dreamy attention.

This is also my pastoral: once a week,
in the apartment above, the prayer group that would chant

for a sustained hour. I never saw them,
I didn't know the words they sang, but I could feel

my breath running heavy or light
as the hour's abstract narrative unfolded, rising and falling

like cicadas, sometimes changing in abrupt
turns of speed, as though a new cantor had taken the lead.

And this, too, is my pastoral: reading in my car
in the supermarket parking lot, reading the Spicer poem

where he wants to write a poem as long
as California. It was cold in the car, then it was too dark.

Why had I been so forlorn, when there was so much
just beyond, leaning into life? Even the cart

humped on a concrete island, the left-behind grapefruit
in the basket like a lost green sun.

And this is my pastoral: reading again and again
the paragraph in the novel by DeLillo where the family eats

the takeout fried chicken in their car,
not talking, trading the parts of the meal among themselves

in a primal choreography, a softly single consciousness,
while outside, everything stumbled apart,

the grim world pastoralizing their heavy coats,
the car's windows, their breath and hands, the grease.

If, by pastoral, we mean a kind of peace,
this is my pastoral: walking up Grand Avenue, down Sixth

Avenue, up Charing Cross Road, down Canal,
then up Valencia, all the way back to Agua Dulce Street,

the street of my childhood, terrifying with roaring trucks
and stray dogs, but whose cold sweetness

flowed night and day from the artesian well at the corner,
where the poor got their water. And this is

also my pastoral: in 1502, when Albrecht Dürer painted
the young hare, he painted into its eye

the window of his studio. The hare is the color
of a winter meadow, brown and gold, each strand of fur

like a slip of grass holding an exact amount
of the season's voltage. And the window within the eye,

which you don't see until you see, is white as a winter sky,
though you know it is joy that is held there.

ON SOME ITEMS IN THE PAINTING BY VELÁZQUEZ

The LASIK-surgery sampling that turns out
    to be the luxury of sound

set deep in the electronica track: just so,
    the mind can follow

the objects back to their bitter
    cartography: the silver tray traced

to the 600 mines and sixty miles of mines
    in the mountain in Potosí,

the workers in loincloth and candlelight:
    or, on the tray, the red cup

the scholars of material culture
    believe to be from Guadalajara,

its clay that gives the water a pleasant
    and fragrant flavor: what

the five-year-old infanta must prefer,
    though it is not desire

her posture telegraphs, but the self-regard
    of someone who understands

she is what economists would call
    a positional good: at twenty-one, married

off in Vienna, she will be dead,
    her body its own consumed

nexus of labor: several miscarriages, four
    children: meanwhile, back in

the immortal childhood, the king
    and queen stand in the mirror,

authority and love, the drapery
    just behind them a silk fabric dyed

red from cochineal, the natives using
    pointed sticks to extract

the dormant bugs from the nopal cactus,
    insects as valuable as silver

and gold: each trophy is taken
    seemingly for granted, except

the objects are in the central axis
    of what Velázquez has organized

in the painting like an exceptional
    identity, where we might pause

and see them, or glance past,
    these silent detonations the world

has collapsed into: like my own desires,
    even though I think

of myself as someone with a regulated
    mind, wanting happiness

as simple as a can of yellow paint,
    or as perfect as the platinum skull

that my fifty million dollars might
    buy, the skull cast by Hirst from

what was once an eighteenth-century head
    and covered with 8,601 diamonds.

EUPHORIC

Maybe I should praise the mapped green
vast where the road I follow disappears

and the GPS triangle that is me begins
to twirl as if I'm not the only one confused

but then follows me into the expanse
in front of the car, in front of the declining sun

that in four hours more or less will glint the humping pump jacks
some oil shade of rusted, and I hope to be gone by then,

to have found some paved road I have never reached
down to touch but will to thank it and whisper *thank you*

like some hostage newly freed and returned to her home
kissed the tarmac in front of cameras before the neck

of her wife or cheek of her father or saluted
some officer obliged to welcome her home,

or I would better show my gratitude today by pulling
down the six coyote carcasses lining the property fence

I shouldn't have entered thinking it was a new way home,
past the gravel pit where kids from Ralls must come to drink

and fuck maybe their older cousins to escape their marriages
or to shoot cans or the sky and someone got so piss-drunk

he took off that pair of green denim jeans so perfect
on the rack at Sears and less so each minute out here

on a road without a name, a path really, and left them crumpled
on the crumpled dirt, the only green in this sea, this ocean of red

earth some still think what they do is farm
and therefore spend their money and hours

disking back and forth across the fields
like boats trawling the Salton Sea or

some astronaut on Mars who lost a special tool
in what wouldn't be called a field but something else

interstellar and spatial like *terra vasta* and this
is Texas so that might work

because the ground is vast and about
to blow around your face and I have

too many lines on mine and I haven't killed
anything with four legs and fur in years

though last night I mis-stepped again
and my friend, the salamander

who clung to the wall near the kitchen
and watched me pass every day since July

jumped beneath a shoe finally and stayed
kissing the floor, as if euphoric,

having finally been released from the wall,
and I buried him in the trash heap I call compost

and I should drive back east to find those carcasses
now bristling in the evening wind and help them back

to the euphoric ground that adored them
and kissed each of their trotting feet.

THREE SKETCHES OF ANXIETY

I've got two hands and an urge
to yank out your teeth,

my lover said, dropping the dress
she made from my shirt

to the floor, *to see the landscape*
a mouth of holes might look like.

Maybe jagged potholes on a rain-
slick street, she said, climbing over

the bed. *Maybe*, she winked, *a prairie*
dog town in West Texas after a flood.

The Cage

Tania James

A t 2:32 AM, the baby falls out of our bed. We decide that night, the baby raging against my chest, that we can never let this happen again.

What if, my husband says, we rearrange the room and push our bed into the corner? Would that look crazy?

We push our bed to the corner of the room and see how crazy it is that we never thought of this before. Two edges of the bed hug the walls. The other two edges we bolt with wooden rails too high for the baby to swing a leg over.

Did you know that a mouse can squeeze itself through the crack beneath a door? Their insides are basically puree, that's how flexible they are. Similarly, our baby pours himself through the space between the rails and achieves a four-point landing.

A mom at the playground weighs in. She's a mom I normally avoid because I can't tell if her nose ring is a nose ring or a mole and it makes me uncomfortable.

I know it sounds crazy, she says, but try making your room *all bed*.

When I ask how, she says she knows a guy.

So the following week my husband and I remove all the furniture from our bedroom and fill the floor with a custom-made, Etsy-sourced foam mattress, delivered by UPS. With the full-floor mattress, our room feels like a spare yet magical pen, granting us the freedom of padded play. We sing our lullabies, beginning with "Twinkle, Twinkle, Little Star," though the baby has no real-life references for stars, having never seen one in our light-polluted skies. Still the baby falls right asleep, and eventually rolls into his own corner. Just as I'm slipping into a dream about our UPS guy, who is sometimes the only guy I see all day other than my husband, the baby whunks his head against a wall.

Here's a crazy idea, my husband says. What if we build some sort of, I don't know, *cage*?

And I'll admit, the cage does look a little crazy at first, but not after we paint the bars a pale sky blue same as the lid, where we fresco clouds in the faint shapes of dinosaurs, whales, and bunnies. The lid of the cage is in fact less cage-like than the actual ceiling of our apartment.

My parents weigh in. We never caged *you*, they say. We let you walk around, dragging a piece of particleboard, partying all night, and when you decided to sleep, you threw down the particleboard and you slept. We also potty trained you when you were fifteen months old and had you swimming laps at two and a half.

What faith my parents had in my ambition and brilliance, they have transferred to the baby. The baby has only to fart into the wind, and they'll say, "Now this one will be a great scholar."

Another night, I fail to notice the baby's escape from the cage until a *WHACK!* rings through the bed frame. I sit up. There he is, grinning pinkly by my bedside. In his hand is a broken piece of sky blue pole.

> Here's a crazy idea, my husband says. What if we build some sort of, I don't know, *cage*?

My husband goes away on a work trip. I imagine him high atop a hotel bed, beneath layers of damask and goose down, sleeping the sleep of the dead.

Did you know that in 1930s London, housewives used to nap their babies in what was basically a wire cage fastened to the outside edges of a tenement window, like an air conditioner, so as to maximize the baby's exposure to fresh air?

For our own open-air compartment, I use a clear acrylic punched with holes and layer it with a mattress and tightly fitted organic cotton sheet. Then I turn to the baby and gesture for him to enter.

The baby says, You must be joking.

I ask the baby if he is my good baby. I ask if he is my good baby or my bad baby.

The baby says he is good.

Then try it, I say.

You try it, he says.

In I go, curling myself into a fetal position that feels better once I stop fighting it. Wow isn't this something, I begin to say, but am interrupted by the bang of the casement windows, which the baby has shut so that I am trapped on all sides.

Classic baby, sharp as a tack. Sharper than I thought.

He trots out the front door and down the steps—Use the handrail! I call out—and up the street, walking jauntily as if to the office, or to my parents' house, where my mother will sit in her rocker and sleep the baby on her chest or on the nearest piece of particleboard.

Twenty floors separate me from the sidewalk below. I'm frightened of the height so I keep my gaze on the scalloped turrets and shingled roofs in my sight line, the laundry lines sagging between windows, a nightgown pinned upside down so that the sleeves are long and pleading. I am finding it difficult to breathe. At some point I notice an open-air compartment just like mine in the window of another apartment building. Inside is a woman curled up, though I can't see the expression on her face, nor can I tell if she sees me. I think, at first, she might be checking her iPhone, but as it turns out, she is flashing her iPhone light at me in a kind of Morse code I can't read but seems something along the lines of I see you.

In the apartment across from that one, there is another open-air compartment, another mother flashing away. Then I see another, and another. Eventually I count more than fifty compartments, all of them made visible by the flashing of lights, each of which seems to convey the same meaning.

Me too   Me too

        Me too   Me too

Me too   Me too

                Me too

At these heights, there is no sound, no fear, only flashing. And it feels good to think that the baby might be looking through my mother's bedroom window, dazzled by all the stars. 🏮

THE EULOGY

Once, you told me about art class
at the cancer center and said sometimes
you start with twelve but end with only nine.
This is common, you shrug and your voice
becomes hoarse and hoarseness is not dread,
it is exhaustion nested in the bottom rung of
your spine and when I am with you,
I feel like a person who hardly knows
how to be a person anymore.

By the Pacific, everyone is trying.
Sand is more beautiful than stars, I say, if you look
under a scope, you can see rhino horns, cacti,
a Peruvian lover. After, you shrug.
After, you die.
After, your father is starting to look thin.
Your friends tend to your grapefruit trees.
Your sister and I sit at a gay bar and don't speak
and someone says to your mother: *It must have been so hard.*

When I hear this, I want to take my fist to a mountain
and pound the surface until five men I have loved
pull me away, and in this dream, they all get along,
and retreat to their separate gardens, where I can visit.
Here, all the gardens are English and all the men
I have loved tell me the things I want to hear except
you, who has no garden, whom I did not enchant,
who says I am an imposter. Tell me all the things
I didn't want to hear. *Narcissist. Liar. Pretty bitch.*
You wouldn't have said any of it, of course.
Even if you had survived.

IN CALIFORNIA, EVERYTHING ALREADY LOOKS LIKE AN AFTERLIFE

—For Leia and Graham

Before he is sick, he surfs the Pacific.
After he is sick, his faint body is pulled
from the water just in time to know
something is expanding. Leia goes over.
Just as friends, she says.
She sleeps in his bed, makes coffee,
tackles the wild zinnias of the Santa Barbara
hills, bends the flora to her spells.
The brain controls everything
except his nearly lifeless foot
moving to a Steely Dan cover.

All his orchids are crooked in the greenhouse
and the cats are missing. *Too many coyotes*,
he once said. When he was well,
everything survived. The orchids grew
erect, the coyotes were spineless, and Leia
stitched things together on her porch
exactly half a mile from the ocean.
Does anyone ever die in California,

I wonder. Leia enshrines him with eucalyptus
and Neruda, calls us, sleeps fetal now in LA.
You want to hear a love story, someone says.
Meaning them. Meaning this thing,
not quite knowable to us, her hand
on his laughing foot, the only part still alive,
it seems, the contract of their intimacy
that is not quite love, not quite
anything we've seen or can name.

Matthew Siegel

BACK HOME BRIAN SHOWS ME A HOME MOVIE

where I am small and powerful as dynamite
in my mother's purse. Strange to see her
loving my father, who looks like me right now.
I snap pictures of the videos with my phone
and show them to her in her tiny kitchen.
She grabs my arm as I swipe through them,
says *slow down* in the voice of a lover
watching their beloved undress for the first time
all over again. She asks why I'm crying and I lie
because it's so beautiful, when really I want to say
because it's no longer ours. I let her console me,
for a moment stop being a man. How many years
since her hand last rubbed my back this way?
When she's gone, this memory will be enough
to crack every bone in my body. It has taken
so much to get me back to her like this: bent,
emptying myself of all I'd been holding back.
Oh, sweet and terrible and perfect this pain,
this love. Finally, I accept it, invite it all in.

I SEE YOU IN THE FIELD OF MY MIND BABY MOO COW

Your look makes me want to jump off the roof
of the modern art museum. How am I supposed
to tell you about my life? Yesterday I saw a turtle
eat a dandelion flower up close. I cannot say what
this might mean to you. It was on my phone,
which is where I've been living lately. I can't expect
you to understand. I cry openly and you stare at me
with big wet cow-eyes. I tell you what the abyss is like.
I heard breathing. It was my own. I wasn't terrified.
Loneliness binds me to myself but I use my phone
as a wedge, use it to keep myself from touching who
I am. Nobody wants to grow up, not even children.
They just want to be taller because they hate being
looked down upon. What is it we see when we turn
and look back? Salt? Pepper? I'll take both. No more
questions. All I want is to sit in this field with you,
little cow, this field I built in my mind. I pet you, make
little noises. You try to move away but I hold on to you,
I throw my arms around your neck. You drop
your dark head, continue chewing what you chew.

EVER THANK GOODNESS

that suddenly you're ok?
Ever consider kissing
the filthy ground? Ever feel
like you're the first person
and maybe the last to say
your own sweet name?
Ever think that maybe all this
shit weather might make us
new? Ever place a hand
over your heart, pledge allegiance
to yourself? Ever feel filled
with harmless filling? Ever
break the surface of yourself?
Ever puke onto paper and send it
to a magazine? Ever bite
a live wire? Ever put metal
in the microwave? Ever take
just five more drinks? Ever
clever yourself into a corner
where you have nothing

but your own empty hands?
Ever break what you just bought?
Ever lose something you can't get back
only to recover and lose it again?
Ever touch your own guts?
Ever imagine yourself
clear as a water glass,
bending like a beam of light?

FICTION

At
the
Center

Delaney Nolan

S hit goes down at The Dream Center. They don't tell you that when you sign up. I was dumb, okay, green, okay. Once or twice a month I found myself sucking gasoline through a rubber tube attached to a can in the back of the car, the gas siphoned out of sleepy curbside trucks. Eddie taught me how, the sly trick, what a brother; a hero, that guy. Imagine a guy who steals gas to go mudding, and then imagine his sister in the passenger seat, shrieking: that's me, that was me, that's how I had fun years before I worked at The Dream Center.

What I did know—what they make clear right off the bat—was that I wasn't going to be working with kids for long. That's intro business. They start you off with kids and then they work you up the ladder to teenagers. What we all know about teenagers is that they're monstrous human beings. Nobody wants to be around them. God knows I didn't.

"What would you like to talk about today, Louis?"

"Talk about suckin' my—"

"Okay, Louis. Lie back down."

I clawed my way into The Dream Center because I was fleeing darker work. Evenings Monday through Friday, mopping the floors at O'Charleys. O'Charleys was a terrible human centrifuge. Sobbing toddlers; citrus degreaser. In May, I watched a man propose to his girlfriend while they sat at a booth, a plate of cheesy baked potato skins between them. I leaned my mop against the bar and clapped. My manager thumbed me toward the back while the girl began to cry. I ate a donut in the walk-in freezer. I read the free newspaper, browsing the six-dollar novena prayers; they all start the same way: O holy St. Anthony, gentlest of saints . . . I went to the Family Dollar and bought all-black clothes for the mopping. I sat in the public library, sending out resumes, scanning the ads from the part-time and ETC sections. Asian egg donors needed. Research trial for bacterial vaginosis. Fun-loving cocktail waitress needed to start ASAP. Send pics.

By Friday my arms would be sore from trying to scrub the stubborn black gunk off the tile, scrubbing and scrubbing under the faintly radio-active light of the wall-mounted menu, its hypersaturated meat products and fluorescent sodas. Then I would dry-vac and gather the scummy water toward me. A curling gunky tide of hair and mud and rice grains washed up at my no-slip shoes.

Oh, I can sing it romantic: mine was a life pressed flush against ten-foot cliffs with its back to the sea, going nowhere, boats at harbor sunk in flames, everybody bailing ship, dead pirates, dead parrots, the captain walking the plank, you get it; what I mean is it was over, for me, my life, my old one, going down. A wreck. The cat ran away. The fiancé left. The cat came back and it died. The fiancé got engaged to a pretty amputee. She could take her leg off and do tricks. Don't tell me about it, I'd tell the ex, when we ran into each other at the Food Lion. I don't want to know. My sister, Dodie, would call me twice a week to check on me and I would lie, lie, lie.

> I clawed my way into The Dream Center because I was fleeing darker work.

When I applied to The Dream Center, I wasn't entirely sure what I was applying for. They asked for good listeners. It was lucky, then, that I'd been practicing to listen all my life. I could smile and nod as men explained things and secretly, without their knowledge or permission, shut down everything behind my face.

They said it was a medical treatment center utilizing new, radical, holistic, blah, blah, blah. I sent another resume. And this time I fibbed like wild: looked up the abbreviations for nursing certificates and medical terminology and psychiatric know-how and spruced it all up. I would learn quick, force myself to be a sharper woman, oh yes, figure out echocardiograms on the fly. I'd learned a thing or two when Eddie was in the hospital (how to read a chart, how to fluff a pillow, ice cubes and bedsores) and I needed this. They called me back. I called my sister and said, *Guess what.*

On the day of my interview, I was greeted by Arthur, friendly guy, sunglasses on his head, smiling big, looking fresh out of a soda commercial. He ushered me into a white office with a white desk and metal cabinets.

He looked over the papers I'd sent, which he'd printed out and put in a folder, now making quiet noises of consideration, a finger crooked over his mouth, little jerking nods. I sat on my hands until my fingers grew dimpled and numb, then folded my hands in my lap.

"Tell me about your experience working with aggressive or resistant clients."

I thought about my ex-fiancé: Daniel, his Skoal, his spitting, his decades-old CD cases on the Jeep floor.

"I've found that in situations with aggressive clients"—I dug my nails into my thumbs to stop my hands from shaking—"it can be helpful to consider their point of view very closely, very very carefully. In fact, I've found it most effective to attempt to erase your point of view—your own thinking—as much as possible, and try to see things from exclusively *their* point of view. Then it's like you're in a maze, the same maze the—client is in, but now there's two of you, and maybe with your heads put together you can find your way out." Arthur clicked his pen on and off. "Or, if you can't find your way out, maybe you can build a lean-to in the maze and just live there." Arthur nodded and wrote several lines in the folder—my folder.

> The crucial fact of the matter is this: dreams are boring. I've no interest in their substance or material.

"Efficiency is an important part of this work." He leaned forward. "We expect to have a high client volume."

"Fantastic."

"Tell me a little bit about your time management skills."

I am very interested in time and its markers "I have several years' experience with triage. Organizing by need and—and making sure patients' needs are assessed quickly, quick as we can, so we can send them on to the doctor. The specialist." *Dry-vac wasting my days and other women my age are out there floating in golden zeppelins of careers, respectable woolen skirts* "I believe my employer's time is as valuable as the patient's." I'd read this online.

Arthur smiled and slapped his knee.

So within a week, presto, there it is, I'm a full-time employee of The Dream Center, and sure there's the teenagers, there's the paperwork, the threats of self-immolation, the horrific waking nightmares that they report day in, day out, unceasingly, in detail, but that's life at TDC—TDC is an acronym, that's jargon. Eddie, buddy, look at me, I'm using jargon these days, I'm a regular professional! We would've gotten a bottle and made a toast; we were always celebrating, and now, at last, when I've got something to celebrate, where have you fucked off to?

Every morning I walk in and see the tired, tired faces around me. The secretary is high as hell on InstaSom. The teenaged clients are surly and nuts, burrowed in their puffed jackets. Nobody wants to be there. Nobody. The mounted television bellows; other people are out there having fun. *Who exactly is this world made for?* the teens all seem to say. *Because it isn't us. It isn't me.*

The crucial fact of the matter is this: dreams are boring. I've no interest in their substance or material. It's healthy for the clients to talk about them, and I've developed a keen listening posture, but dreams are basically all the same and I'm mostly tuned out at this point. Something attacks you, or you're embarrassed in school, or you're chasing your little brother who is running into traffic but your legs don't work, your teeth fall out, your arms won't lift: there's a great deal of paralysis. I listen and prescribe. Talk all they like, most of the clients are long-term whacked, and only sleep will fix them; sleep meds, tranqs, Valium, lullabies, warm compresses, quilts, baths, a sneaky nip of vodka, three hours on the treadmill, whatever it takes to knock them out.

The idea is this: a couple of years ago, when the FDA approved InstaSom, it slowly emerged that about two percent of users have a delayed and extreme reaction. They get a kind of dream backlog, is how it's described on the internet, and it's awful for their health, just awful for the people around them who have to witness it, and after that guy in Florida tried to cram his niece down the garbage disposal the government put up some funding right quick for a few centers to treat the screwballs. I am good at this; or rather, I can pass as competent, and I shuffle the kids through, help them transition back to full-on sleeping, with few complaints, until it's all practically automated: I can do this with my eyes closed.

Six months into the job, a girl comes in: Greta. Like most of them, she has a pinched, dour look, and sits on the end of the couch farthest from me. I've got my own office here. It hasn't got my name on the door, but everyone knows it's mine. I've placed a Brazilian philodendron on the windowsill. I remember to water it once every couple of months, and it is still alive. It is alive. The ladder: I'm on its rungs.

"Well, Greta," I start, "what seems to be the trouble?"

And Greta retches all over the floor in front of her feet, which isn't so unusual; I buzz for the custodian. I lead Greta into a conference room at the end of the hall to try again, and here we are, the tiny invisible trophy I spin in my head: some other woman now carries the mop, amen.

Everybody thinks it's real cute, not sleeping. They take their InstaSom once a day and nobody sees the ones with the bad reactions—nobody does except us; teens get embarrassed; their friends don't sleep, their teachers, their parents, their magazine heroes. Nobody.

There is, I'm told, an incredible amount of money to be made with InstaSom, just unimaginable stacks; it isn't merely about the drug but also about worker productivity, people holding two jobs since they don't have to clock out and sleep, and I've heard this in turn fixes outsourcing, and corporate taxes, and then there's an awful lot of financial numbers to con- sider, the stock market, petrol, maybe, I couldn't tell you exactly, et cetera, et cetera, but the point at the end of the day is that it's more efficient for everybody if we treat those who can't handle the drug, rather than remove InstaSom from shelves. Good news for me.

The Dream Center is a brick building on the side of a state highway, sand- wiched between a Food Lion and a cash-for-gold place that I suspect is a front for Russian mobsters. Women younger than me are always walking out of that place in floor-length fur coats.

You're beautiful, I tell them, on my way into work at 7:00 AM as they pass me in the parking lot. That fur, I say, is it real?

They smile and nod in a way that indicates they do not speak English. I love the Russians. I speak to them at every opportunity. I step out for smoke breaks and jabber in their ear until they sink their bleached hair and frosty lips deep inside their fox fur collars.

"I been seein' shit." Greta is slouched in the rolling chair on the other side of the conference table, jerking the seat from side to side by swinging her legs. I tap my pen against my lips and nod.

"Can you tell me about the shit?"

Greta sits up and leans forward. She's got those stiff, White Rain bangs that are cut sharp to end just at her brows, and they twitch every time she blinks. A belly button piercing peeks out below the hem of her shirt. There are, of course, deep blue circles of exhaustion beneath her eyes. She is very pretty, Greta, blond and thick, and I get the impression that she would excel at being cruel to me and I very much do not want her to make fun of me. This is my problem: I cannot separate the teens of my youth from the teens of the present.

"*Sexual*. Shit. People whispering—*pussy, wanna fuck. Sugartits.*"

I nod. I look down at her folder. *Three months InstaSom 1x day* says the intake form. *Client reports waking terrors. Primary complaint: extensive auditory hallucinations.* Greta is trying to embarrass me. The trick, when they do that, is to take them absolutely seriously.

"Sugartits," I repeat. "Does that upset you?"

"My mom," Greta continues, "she takes food out the refrigerator. She hides it underneath the bed and eats in secret."

"Oh." I can't tell whether this is a dream or not.

"When I was a little kid," she says, "my momma would take food from the fridge into her room. She would hide it 'neath the bed and eat and eat and eat in secret."

"You told me that," I say.

"My daddy," she goes on, "he spit on a piece of paper"—her voice breaks—"and he mailed the piece of paper to me." She puts her head in her hands. "We lived in the same house."

> And Greta retches all over the floor in front of her feet, which isn't so unusual; I buzz for the custodian.

"Oh." I'd like to say we're building a rapport, but we aren't.

Greta goes limp and stares at the floor. I wait. Outside, the one ice of the year is turning to thick brown sludge. January in Fayetteville has nothing to offer. It gets cold and wet and then it hangs around. If it snows an inch, half an inch, everybody loses their mind; drivers go careening off the highway and blitz themselves on the guardrail. I think sometimes what it'd be like if I were a real doctor. IVs of saline, sending the fixed ones home to their families. *What's the trouble?* I'd say, snapping on latex gloves. Cupping some dumb baby's face in my hand, some kid mashed up by a drunk driver. *You're going to be okay.*

"Other things, too," Greta says. She looks at her nails while she talks, little plastic rhinestones winking. "One day I was walking down the hallway. And then I feel it . . ." She hesitates. "My body parts falling off. First my nose. I reach up to touch my face. But it ain't there. And my lips, too, like they been cut off but then healed up again, so it's only just a scar. Nothin' there. No nose. No lips. I start pattin' my face all over, scared. Then I look at my hands." Greta holds her hands out flat, palms up. "And there, too, my fingers gone, like somebody's chopped 'em right off at the knuckle. So then I fall down, because my toes, and my feet, they gone. I'm slappin' at my head with my messed-up hands, because my ears are gone, like I'm this cripple, this freak, right in the middle of the hallway, on the tile, trying to drag myself away—I dunno where I thought I'd get to—with my stump arms, trying to yell but my voice all crazy because I got no lips, no tongue. Screaming and screaming. My body parts falling off. And then Mrs. Dunhill is there, shaking me, trying to get me okay. But I keep touching my face. Because I can't see my own face. So I can't be for sure that it's all still there." She looks up and then slouches deeper into her office chair, spreads her legs and throws her hands into her lap, like now that she's said it out loud, I own the rights. I reach to pat her on the knee but she flinches and I pull back.

> Daniel used to feel sorry for me, I think, like he feels sorry for the amputee.

I recommend a sleeping aid and send her to the Rite Aid on the corner. This is classic InstaSom sickness, I tell her. Classic. Wean yourself off it. Take it every other day. Then twice a week. Then stop.

At home, in my apartment, I cook the fine and wholesome food I can now afford to buy. Fish. Green leaves. Rice. I eat off a white plastic plate, sitting on the couch.

I call my sister. My sister's a veritable goddamn angel. Dodie spends three months out of the year in Haiti, Jamaica, the DR—one of those hot islands where children are being crushed by dengue and political ill will. She sends out Christmas cards where she's sitting on her heels in her doctor's lab coat, grinning crazily, sweating, half strangled by the arms of a doting child. Next year, same lab coat, different kid.

"Dodie," I say, when she picks up the phone. I check the clock—it's late, even later than I thought.

"Beatrice. What in the hell?"

"It's crazy, isn't it? Three years today."

And she's silent. I've got her. She was about to scold me—scold!—for calling her so late, but right at the crucial moment I sprung the anniversary on her. Three years ago Eddie died. He was sick for a long time, so the *specific* day doesn't seem like it ought to matter, but of course it does. I can feel the day ribboned underneath the other days, like a hard, tumorous node beneath the skin that doesn't go away with time.

"What are you doing?" she asks.

"Salsa dancing."

"You should've called earlier. I already put the girls to bed."

"Tell them Aunt Beatrice says *cheerio*." We'd recently watched *Mary Poppins*.

"You should come over this weekend. For dinner."

But this feels somehow unfair, her reaching out to me. As it turns out, the size of my heart is so small, that it takes nothing—practically nothing at all—to be the better woman.

"Okay. Maybe. I'll call." I put my head against the cool wood of the doorjamb. Sure, I'd like to say something about Eddie. But what can I say? Nothing over the phone, not now—into the mouth of the dumb plastic phone. "How are they? The girls."

"They're good; they miss you. They ask after you. Come by this weekend and see for yourself."

Yes, yes, I say. Sure I will, yes.

My ex-fiancé is slumped at the door of the office building when I arrive the next morning, breathing on my hands as I walk across the wide cold lot. It's freezing, just getting light. The parking lot is almost empty, except for his truck, parked crooked. The neon light in the Russians' store is blinking CASH, CASH, CASH. The file folders with clients' records have started overflowing from the cabinets so I keep a few in my car now. They fill the back seat, slide onto the floor mats. When I get my purse from the passenger seat, a yellow sheet of notes flies away, snapping in the wind. Across the expressway are three shuttered shops, right in a row, the third one gutted by fire. This part of Fayetteville has gotten pretty neglected. Fort Bragg has expanded, built its own little shopping area across town, and so business has mostly moved elsewhere; there's plenty of places for it to go—if you were an optimist, maybe that'd cheer you.

"Beatrice," he groans, drunk and sleepy. "Beatrice."

"Go home, huh?" Every few months he turns up and acts like we have some kind of heartbreak to resolve. I used to get real excited—thinking sweetness, violins, *he's changed his mind, returned*, maybe a lovely tear, fingertips on the lips, oysters and pearls and sugar on the toast, but be real; it never turns out that way. No champagne on the boat deck for us. We get vodka and zit cream, nursing weltschmerz like a junkie in your underwear on the tiled floor. Daniel used to feel sorry for me, I think, like he feels sorry for the amputee. And sure, I want more attention. But it isn't flattering. It just makes me sad now.

"I've got it. That InstaSom sickness." He reaches out and plucks at my shoelaces as I stand before him. He blinks, a little unevenly. "I've got— you've got to—"

"No, you don't," I say.

"Beatie, I'm sick. I'm suck—I'm sick as a fucking dog, Beat."

Gingerly, I brush him away from the front door. I fish around for my keys. "You haven't got any disorder," I say. "Not the kind we treat here. Go home."

"I'm going to die," he wails.

"Yes," I agree. "We are." I close the door behind me.

Greta's back. Her mouth pops open and closed like a fish's.

"How are you feeling?" I ask. My computer buzzes in its sleep. Heels click smartly down the hall outside my closed office door. It's been two weeks since I saw Greta. I thought she'd been cured. The fluorescent lights, the lowered blinds, the painted cinder-block walls—they all make me feel skinned alive, like I've just crawled out of a fire that took off the top dermal layer, something second-degree, and the room hurts everywhere it touches. I offer Greta some water.

"Thanks. I'm fine."

"Still having hallucinations?"

She shrugs. I click my pen.

"That's fine," I say. "Cutting back on the InstaSom?"

She lifts her chin, once, and lets it drop heavily to her chest. She seems subdued, somehow. Maybe tired. It's weird, adjusting to the sleeping world. Or I hear it is. I've never taken the drug myself. I look down at my notes. I haven't written anything. "Waking dreams still messing with you? You can tell me about them. If you want to."

She snorts.

"How's your family?" I try. "Have you got any brothers? Sisters?"

"My sister," she says, "last night she turned into a toad. She made fun of me for sleepin'. Then she chained me to the radiator."

"That's funny," I say, "my brother used to call me Toad." Greta stares. "Eddie, my brother," I add. "He's dead. He died." Greta just waits. "So you've been sleeping?"

Greta pinches her fingers together and peers at me through them. A thimbleful, she seems to be saying. A drop of sleep. "I wake up: my bed's on fire."

I clear my throat and try starting over. "How have you been?"

"I'm standing in the street," she says. "It's dark. It's warm. The houses are dark. My face is dark. I hear the little crucifer frogs cry and cry. I hear a knocking on the asphalt." I jot notes. Greta's face is transfixed, like she's touched an electric current. "I can't see where it comes from. I try to walk away from it. The street rolls into blackness. But then I see. There's a woman. She sits on top of a black horse. The horse walks toward me. The woman has no arms. She wants to make a noise. She wears a cloth over her face. A dark hood. The horse's ears have been cut off. Cut flat to the skull. Its mane has been cut off too, and its tail. Black oil covers its back where the woman sits. It slides along the horse's side. It drips onto the asphalt. I see the dripping. The horse comes closer. It opens its jaw and closes it.

> It's weird, adjusting to the sleeping world. Or I hear it is.

Very tall. The only thing I can see. Like a spotlight glares on it. I can't hear the dripping anymore. I can't move. The eyes roll in the terrible face. The hooves are sharp on the asphalt. I see the sutures where the woman's arms have been cut off. She leans toward me."

Greta stops. She blinks and her face relaxes. I watch her, my pen still over the blank paper, while she digs gum out of her pocket and unwraps it. "Will you get me a glass of water?" she asks.

I stand in the office kitchenette for a long time with the water glass. The counter is dirty yellow Formica I scratch with a nail. Who the hell dreams like that? But yet, the dream is somehow deeply satisfying—I hear this stuff all the time, these waking dreams, these insomnia visions, but this one might be my all-time favorite. I can locate within myself the same nightmare feeling: standing alone in the road, bewildered, while mutilation presents itself. I have a crazy thought: that Greta is my best friend. My only friend. When I get back with her water, she's gone.

I go that weekend for dinner with Dodie. Her kids—my nieces—are eight and four, excited about nearly everything for at least a few seconds at a time. They twist maniacally in their chairs, pulling at their cheeks, singing to their green beans. I make faces, pretend to choke when Dodie goes to the kitchen for more wine. I claw at my throat and make big eyes at the older girl.

"Babbit," I say, using the nickname I made up for her, "I think my salad's poisoned."

"No, it's not." She giggles.

"Sure, it is. Taste it."

The kid reaches across the table, half climbing onto it, and picks up a leaf with her fingers. She eats it, watching me, waiting for cues, and when my eyes bug out she tries to make hers big too, spluttering spinach and red wine vinegar everywhere, collapsing in a hysterical bubbly fit. The littler one, Debbie, watches us, laughing at our laughing.

> Pretty Dodie: she got the good stuff television promised us.

"Beatrice, please," Dodie says from the doorway. Dodie is always standing in doorways saying please. She sounds tired, but that's impossible. Dodie's InstaSommed up to her eyeballs.

"Why are you trying to kill us?" I squeak, and half collapse out of my chair, driving Babbit and Debbie wild with joy. They hop up out of their chairs and swarm over to me, pretend-choking, until we three lie on the ground in imitation of a pile of corpses, twitching and filling the dining room with our death rattles. Dodie's husband, Seojun, sticks his head in the door, rubs his eyes, and ducks out immediately back to work.

Poor, sweet Dodie. She covers her face with her hands.

After dinner we clear the table while the girls sit on the couch, coweyed and hypnotized in front of the first *Toy Story*.

"I worry about you," Dodie is saying. Her hands flutter around nervously. She stacks her bowls in the cupboard gently enough that they don't make a sound. She's never been great with loud noises, the big and startling. When I drop the grater too roughly in the drawer I half expect her to fly away.

"What for?"

"Have you been drinking?"

"Not particularly." Dodie looks over her shoulder at me when I say it, but it's the truth.

"You seem so—I don't know, unfocused, lately."

"What would I be focusing on?" I snap out a cloth napkin.

"Well, your career?" She shakes her head and places both hands flat on the counter. "Listen, Beatrice. I want you to stop showing up at the girls' school in the middle of the day. It confuses them. They're always begging me to bring you around. You can't be taking them out for lunch all the time or whatever." She takes the napkin from me and wads it in her skinny hand. "I don't want to do this, but I'm going to rescind permission for you to sign them out if you don't quit it."

Pretty Dodie: she got the good stuff television promised us. She is lovely, small-boned, has a wonderful family, an adoring husband; her life is challenging and fulfilling. And she makes this look easy, the way beauty works best. It is so natural and simple on her, this beauty, this happiness. When I was young, I would pour over the advertisements and magazines and feel so happy that I would look like the beautiful women one day. I was like a vase filled right up to the brim with joy. It was natural that I should someday be beautiful. It appeared so easy. I did not receive the bounty that was promised, but Dodie held it always and that is nearly enough.

When I don't answer, she asks, "Have you talked to Daniel lately?"

"He showed up outside my office again this week."

She stops and the plate she's holding droops at her side. "Oh, Beatrice."

"It's fine. It doesn't bother me anymore." Also mostly true. I drop forks tine-down in the drying rack. "It's fine." She's still making dopey eyes at me.

She sighs and raises an eyebrow as she plunges the plate back into the sink. She looks very much like our mother. "Well. It's nice to hear you're going to your office on time."

"Come on."

"Sorry." She hands the dish to me to dry, staring at the dish instead of my face, and she smiles. "You know—Eddie would've loved that job. God, he would've loved to hear about that job."

And I smile. Because that's true, that's certainly true—it seems right up Eddie's alley, the idea of listening to teenagers' weird dreams. He was a graphic designer, an oddball. Once, he made life-sized felt puppets for Babbit and Debbie, the puppets tailored and colored to look like them: one with curly red hair, one just a little baby, the size of a watermelon. She has reminded me of this. At that moment, I love Dodie so much that I cannot stand it; I want to lock us both in a closet forever, until the world is safe, the two of us smothered by coats. "Yeah."

"He would've told us the craziest stories," she says. Meaning that I don't—I fail to craft the anecdotes. "How is it, anyway?"

"What?"

"How's work?"

Which is it, all it ever comes down to with Dodie and me, always the end of our conversations, efficiency and careers but we never can finish talking about "Work is work, money is money, I'd rather be on a yacht gettin' some dick but here I am, Dodie, Jesus," at which she slaps the dishrag on the counter and that's it, there, that's where we finish.

I go into the living room while I wait for her to send Seo-jun to kick me out. I put my arms around the girls and bury my face in Babbit's hair. She smells like hotel soap and it is so nice; it is so, so nice. The tiny cowboy is crying before us. All I want is to be able to look at the bottom of my shoe and see my name, or the name of the person who owns me.

I take the bus home. I take a bottle of red from Dodie's wine rack before I leave and hold it in between my legs, trying to push the cork down with my thumb. By the time I get to my house it's mostly gone. Every house on the block is alive with light, every window blazing. It's 3:00 AM, and my neighbor is weeding his garden under the floodlights. I lift my hand in greeting. When I go to bed, I'll be the only one sleeping for miles around. Once I get inside, I jab the bottle through the living room window.

We went mudding, once. Maybe ten years back, before InstaSom, before Daniel, when Eddie was about to start working at a studio and Dodie was still single. We took Dodie's Jeep—she hadn't traded in for a van yet—out to a track near St. Mere. Dodie was worried because her Jeep wasn't lifted any. "Take it easy," she kept saying. "Don't bottom out." We ramped up through some bog and slammed the bumper down into the chewed-up trails. Eddie was driving, and I was in the passenger seat, screaming laughing. The windows went thick with mud while the tires spun. We slid around while smoke came out the wheel well. There's nothing really that can hit you but the ground, so even though it feels dangerous sometimes, you're safe inside. I open my phone and push the numbers very carefully and deliberately.

"Yes, hello?" I say. My voice is clear as a bell. Someone should record me singing, I think. I should be an opera singer. I should practice fluctuating the tone of my voice, testing its registers. "Yes. Someone has broken my window."

"Where are you, ma'am?"

I look down at my feet. The last of the wine has run down my arm and into my shoes. The 911 operator is very patient. "I am inside," I say.

"Are you in immediate danger?"

I curl up on the couch with the bottle tucked between the cushions. The fabric leaves the shape of diamonds on my cheek. I'm the only one sleeping for miles, dropped into a blank, inkwell void where Eddie still isn't. When the police knock on the door I have to concentrate on their faces, on smiling. No, officer. Thank you. Everything here is fine.

Two weeks later, Daniel calls me at the office to apologize. He's getting sober, again, he says. He says he wants to make amends. I can hear the amputee in the background, yelling at him to hang up. I hang up. The secretary hollers from the lobby.

Greta is back, which is odd, because usually people don't come in for so many sessions. She sits in my chair, tying rubber bands together to form a long chain.

"How have you been?" I ask. "You should be all fixed up by now."

She shrugs. I ought to wait for her to talk but I haven't got the patience today.

> I want to lock us both in a closet forever, until the world is safe, the two of us smothered by coats.

"You seem much better. You look well-rested. Can you answer a few simple questions? Can you tell me what month it is?"

Greta looks at me like I'm demented. "Um, it's *February*."

"That's right."

"The worst month."

"That's right." I keep waiting. Greta's skin is bright now; her fingers move cannily among the rubber bands. She finishes a chain and wraps it around a wrist, admires her arm. She will live a long, happy life, I think, or else she won't. I look at the clock. We still have twenty-six minutes left in our appointment block. "Do you miss the extra time you got with InstaSom? That's a common complaint." People have nightmares about it—waking up to find that their children are grown, the world has fixed itself while they were gone, everyone has grown up happy and well-mannered without them. "We can prescribe something for that."

"No, no."

"Hallucinations?"

"Did you ever have a family?"

"Listen, this isn't psychotherapy," I say, a little snippy.

"I miss my family," she says. "They love me. They just love me so much."

"They're right out in the hallway," I say warily.

"It's just I feel sorry for *them*. For the people still taking it. Do you take it?"

"No."

"Why?"

I put my pen down and lean in toward Greta. I crook my finger. She leans in. "You want to know why?"

She nods.

And I start to say, *Because I'm not an asshole*, but the words dig their nails in somewhere in my throat, and I find I'm choking, ugly-crying in a terrible way, absolutely lousy with snot. I reach out for Greta's hand, and she flinches away at first but then lets me take it. She is quiet for a minute, but then chatters on over the sound of my choking, patting my hand as I take creepy, shuddering breaths.

"I just can't imagine it, now that I'm all recovered and sleepin' again," she's saying. "I feel real sorry for them. It's bonkers! Not even a nap? All these people, up awake all night. How can you keep it together when you know what's goin' on all the time? Like—how can you stand it, not being able to give up at least once a day?" Greta shakes her head and her stiff blond bangs twitch across her forehead. I love Greta.

I put my hand over hers over mine. I pat her hand. I reach to give her the Kleenex, as though I'm the one who's helping.

When I get home, the sun's out. The lindens are brown and shivering. Scummy slush is all over the sidewalk, and it reminds me of the dry-vac. Never again, I think to myself. I'll never be at the mercy of a dry-vac again. Never at the mercy of anything.

There's a card for me in the mail. It's from Dodie. There's no stamp on it. It must have been dropped into my mailbox by hand. I look around like she might be spying on me, but there's nobody. I rip open the envelope.

It's a birthday card. It's my birthday. Today I am thirty-six.

Babbit and Debbie made me the card. It is on pink construction paper and covered in big heart stickers. Dodie wrote *Happy Birthday Aunt Beatrice!* in curly script, and Babbit has written her name. Debbie has scribbled a wild tangle of marker lines. She pressed so hard into the paper that the ink has bled right through. It's a spindly blue nest on the pink paper. On the opposite side of the card, Babbit has drawn three stick figures, one taller than the other two. Each has a macrocephalous head and long limbs and a huge, frightening smile. They have their arms around one another and look out at me.

The card is that thing again, that thing I save for Dodie and the television cowboy: beautiful. It is fucking perfect. I say out loud, to nobody: "It is fucking perfect." I say out loud what I said to Daniel right before he left: "Oh I never, ever, ever, ever, ever, ever, ever want to have kids." I rip each sticker off. I drop them one by one. I walk inside. I close the door. I stand in the front hall and try not to move.

The problem, you see, is that the real meaning of the word *heart* is not what people think. It is not candy. It is staples puckered across a dark purpling chest. It means fleshy, white pulp, snipped by metal tools under bright lights. Thick plastic breathing tubes stuck up out of orange iodined skin. The corner of the mouth pulled aside for the breathing tube to fit in. It is Eddie as thick, pale, hideous meat, the stuff that dogs eat. It is the exhausted, repetitive labor of living. There's no room for sweetness. There should be another word for it. *Heart* is a word like butterflies and Sunday mornings; even *cardiology*, *cardiogram* are too close to a valentine. A black horse. A dreamless sleep. I don't know what the new word ought to be. I go into the kitchen. I drop my bag. My brother is dead. My brother is dead. That's it. 🏛

EVASIVE ME

Of course there's a certificate, bleeding
carbon at the creases and impressions,

detailing my metrics and lineage the night
I entered the earthly air in a new hospital

built by the intricate partnership between
Rust Belt governance, capitalism

and Christ, though I lie to people I like,
saying I was born in a garden so near

the sea that my mother—multilingual
and remarkably tall—rinsed me at the fringe

of the tide the morning after labor,
the horizon cloudless and birdless

while the sand whispered spells of protection,
depth, and solemnity upon the pair of us,

and amid this farce my dear listeners
don expressions of distrust or ire

as likely they should, faced with evasive
me, so wearied even before boyhood

by the truth that I've forever disallowed
my ears and my mouth any songs not made

from the water, dirt, wind, salt, and fire
of American manipulation.

ASHTRAY

Filling with my mother's smolderings,
this tawny, six-sided, three-pound glass dish
has sat forty years at the table's center.
During lapses in labor or happiness
mother smoked Merit after Merit, her mind
a crowded parlor of plans, self-hate,
and urgent glimpses of encounters long past.
She split the skin atop my father's skull
once with this ashtray as he grabbed her.
Weekly, after she emptied and washed it, Friday's light
entered the drafty sash and upheld this ashtray
as the crown of one woman's quiet country.

GOODALE PARK

A hunched man speaks Korean to the geese,
feeding them old bread at the pond brim
while much of the park late April
is a unified green breathing.
When the clusters of ducks bob
backward from submergence, their beaks look
lacquered, and they shimmy their wings
as if deflecting mortality.
A tall can of common beer in a paper sleeve
does now for me what the burgeoning season does
for the ducks; the yeasty froth and the slight sting
imbue some peace after a year of grieving
a brother who, in youth, screamed elatedly
when our mother, her eyes widened and softened
by codeine, first showed us how to draw
frenzies of the large, long-traveled birds
by tossing pieces of stale sourdough
onto the edge of the park's dark water.

Ross White

FROM MONEY

my parents used the term *from money*   it meant a lineage
but I envisioned a woman emerging naked and fully formed

from sierras of unmarked bills   there was no derision
in the term but an understanding that she was not like us

she had not worked a day in her life   she had never worn mittens
with holes in them   her house had central heat instead of a wood stove

she knew how to shuck an oyster   always knew which fork
was appropriate   there was a lot we knew that she could not

but it was understood that these were Pandora kinds of knowledge
I asked if it was better to not have money   then have it but they said

it was more elegant to come *from money*   the *nouveau riche*
they said suffered *from the one great affliction*   *a lack of manners*

I said *it doesn't seem like the bad kind of suffering*   they said
you're too young to know what shame is   *but you know* I said

they argued behind the closed bedroom door once about a prostitute
I envisioned the prostitute   naked on sheets

of crisp hundred dollar bills I understood even then that money
and sex were cousins though the order of the transaction confused me

the art of the deal how to get what you want
withhold whatever has value my father kept secret

that he was starting another family we could have
with a little detective work sleuthed it out rule number one

follow the money people will do terrible things to get it
my half brother was born no— he was practically minted

TEATIME IN DARJEELING

Ann Tashi Slater

A Tasseography for the Past

I.

Every morning in Tokyo, as the tile roofs of the neighborhood houses come into view, I put the kettle on for Darjeeling tea. When the water reaches a rolling boil, I pour it over the dark, crinkly leaves of the *Camellia sinensis* var. *sinensis* tea plant. Like the Japanese paper flowers Proust writes of, the ones that bloom when put in water, a world unfolds as the leaves steep and the musky, floral fragrance rises.

The tea estates, which I first saw as a small girl when my mother brought her American husband and children to her hometown of Darjeeling, lie 6,700 feet in the Himalayas near the India-Tibet border. The long, even rows of emerald tea bushes undulate with the hills, dirt paths cutting through them like veins. The estate names read like a roster of champion racehorses: Margaret's Hope, Makaibari, Happy Valley, Rangaroon, Liza Hill. The teas include crisp and ethereal First Flush, harvested in spring; rough-edged Rain Tea, produced during the summer monsoon; fruity, coppery Autumn Flush.

Bringing water to a boil, waiting for the leaves to brew, pouring the tea into a cup and milk into the tea (only a drop, so the taste isn't diluted), I'm doing what my Tibetan family has done for over a century. The earthy notes of the amber liquid conjure the wool-and-camphor smell of our Darjeeling house, the odor of butter lamps and incense in the altar room. They make me feel connected to the land itself: 28,000-foot Mount Kanchenjunga, soaring over the town; sacred Observatory Hill, where our family feasted at Losar New Year; the dusky waters of the Teesta River, where my grandparents' ashes were scattered.

> There was another reason I wanted nothing to do with the Asian part of me.

2.

I was born in Spain, when my father was stationed at an American naval base in Andalusia. I spent my first two years there, lived with my grandparents in Darjeeling while my parents got settled in Nepal for an assignment with the Peace Corps, and then moved to the States when I was three. For twenty years, I didn't visit India or think much about it. Not wanting her children to feel different from the other kids—and thrilled to leave behind the old country—my mother made no effort to educate us about her culture of origin. She was determined to do things *à la American*, as she liked to joke. She did cook curries and call me "darling" in the British accent she acquired at convent school in Darjeeling, but she'd put aside the long Tibetan *chuba* dress in favor of slim wool suits and swing dresses, pencil skirts and capri pants.

She went all out at Christmas, decorating a tree with twinkling lights and home-made gingerbread men, filling the living room with presents. At Easter there was an egg hunt, and on Halloween, trick-or-treating in the costumes she'd stayed up night after night sewing. My intellectual psychiatrist father, whom she met when they were medical school classmates at Columbia, objected to these pursuits as mindless adherence to social convention, but I sided with my mother because I loved the presents and egg hunts and costumes.

The best part, though, about not having to wear Tibetan dress or celebrate Losar New Year in February was that no one knew I was half-Tibetan. In 1960s and '70s New Jersey and California, there were relatively few children of Asian descent, and I lay awake at night wishing for blond hair and blue eyes. It was bad enough that I had to endure taunts on the playground of "Ching, Chong, Chinaman!" I didn't need people finding out that I actually came from some strange place they'd never heard of. My plain vanilla name, Ann Davis, kept its secrets, but because I looked different, people tried to guess my ethnicity: "Hawaiian? Irish? Italian?" And if I told them I was born in Spain: "Oh, that's it. Spanish."

There was another reason I wanted nothing to do with the Asian part of me. By nature, and coming of age during the era of Betty Friedan and Gloria Steinem, I was an outspoken, strong-willed girl. My father encouraged these traits, exhorting me not to "trivialize" myself, to consider myself anyone's equal. But in my mother's Tibetan-by-way-of-the-British-Raj upbringing, girls were socialized to be demure and humble; I was, she fretted, becoming "too American." *Don't ask so many questions!* she'd say when we argued. *Don't talk so much! Who do you think you are?* A good question, I always felt, though not in the way she intended. I brooded over the meaning of "half-Tibetan" and "half-American."

My parents divorced when I was eleven. Though my mother and I continued to clash throughout my teen years, I became her confidante. On weekends, we'd sit at breakfast long after my siblings had finished and she'd talk about her job as director of a public health clinic. She told stories about the dorm parties she threw in medical school ("We drank loads of Japanese sake and then rumbaed down the hall!"); about going on pilgrimage from Darjeeling to Bodh Gaya with her family by overnight rail and waking to the sun rising over the Indian plain. Filled with remorse that I'd looked at her only as "mother," I felt the first stirrings of wanting to know more about where she'd come from.

When it was time to leave home, I was afraid my mother would be lonely, but I also knew she wanted me to set forth into the world as she had. In college, I studied comparative literature, focusing on French and Latin American novels, and decided to make my life as a writer in Paris. But the confusion and anxieties of my girlhood persisted, my unhappiness intensified by a letter from my mother during senior year: she'd raised me all wrong, she was sorry to say; in the end, I *had* turned out "too American." After graduating, I fell into a depression. For reasons I couldn't fathom, I abandoned my Paris plan and went to Darjeeling, winging my way back like a homing pigeon to the country I'd last seen when I was three.

Until the moment I arrived, I worried I was making a terrible mistake. Why travel to the place that seemed like the source of my melancholia?

Being in Darjeeling for the first time as an adult—visiting the house where my mother grew up and the old monasteries where our family prayed—I felt like an archaeologist stumbling across the excavation site I'd long been searching for. Since tea is such an integral part of my Tibetan family's life, it's deeply entwined with my experience in Darjeeling. When I tried tea as a girl, I recoiled from the astringent flavor. Yet in Darjeeling I began drinking it and have continued ever since. The tea ritual, its complex materiality, has changed the way I feel about my family, my mother, and myself.

> When I tried tea as a girl, I recoiled from the astringent flavor.

PHOTO: TENKI DAVIS

3.
Tea plants were introduced to Darjeeling in the mid-1800s by Dr. Archibald Campbell, a Scot working for the East India Company to develop the remote, sparsely inhabited area as a retreat from the sweltering plains in summer. The plants flourished in the high-altitude rain, mist, and sun, and the local tea industry was born, transforming the town into a cosmopolitan crossroads of Europeans, Anglo-Indians, Tibetans, Nepalis, Chinese, and Bengalis. My great-great-great-grandfather worked as an assistant to Campbell and sold family land for the founding of the Pandam and Glenburn tea estates. In the 1920s, my great-grandfather bought the Aloobari estate, site of Campbell's first tea-planting experiments. The estates were wild and lonely places, vast tracts where mostly

British tea planters—often working-class men low in the pecking order—oversaw the laborers who plucked the leaves. Though tea was a constant reminder to the laborers of the disparity between their meager wages and the profitability of the estates, they drank cup after cup on the job and at home, adding salt or milk and sugar. And with millions of pounds produced annually, tea became indispensable to the British Raj and local elites at the center of Darjeeling social life, enjoyed at tennis parties and in ladies' drawing rooms, at the Gymkhana Club, and the New Year's tea given by His Excellency the Governor of Bengal.

For my family, tea became as essential as daily prayers. In the half century my grandparents lived at Annandale, their house on a quiet side street, they had tea every day at four. It was a time to relax and reconnect before going back to the Windamere, their Raj-era hotel, and preparing for the evening's events.

When I returned after college, my grandfather was gone. Then, and during visits over the years, as I settled in Tokyo, married, and became a university professor, I had tea in the living room with my grandmother. *Thangka* scroll paintings hung on the walls, renderings of landscapes and heavenscapes with jeweled trees and palaces, buddhas and flying monks, yogis and demons. In one corner were photos of Queen Elizabeth and the Thirteenth Dalai Lama; in another, my grandparents' collection of Gershwin records. The tea items were laid out with the same care as the family's ritual prayer objects were arranged in the altar room: teapot with tea cozy, sugar bowl, creamer of heated milk; Wedgwood Campion flower-patterned china.

Some of these items dated back to the early 1900s, when my grandmother was a girl. After her mother died, she supervised the household staff in serving tea to the officials constantly calling on my great-grandfather, who was active in local politics and worked with the Dalai Lama. She saw to it that the sterling tea service was polished, the linen napkins starched, fragrant roses arranged in bowls, finger sandwiches cut into perfect triangles and arrayed on doily-covered platters, cakes and tarts set out on tiered stands. "How many people came," she liked to remember. "Viceroys, rajas and ranis, ambassadors. Big people, short people, mad people. My father had full reliance on me, small as I was!" I saw in her the same pride my mother took in preparing a meal or knitting a sweater, and was struck by how my grandmother and mother didn't feel diminished by these woman-identified acts. Maybe this was part of what my mother had wanted me to understand when she pushed me to be more demure and humble.

As my grandmother and I talked, the peaks of Kanchenjunga fading to blue in the oncoming twilight, we drank cup after cup of tea. We ate Scottish Walkers Shortbread and syrupy Indian *rasgulla* cottage cheese and semolina balls, Sikkimese *gram* (fried chickpea flour with turmeric and cumin) and peanut butter "imported from California" (brought by my mother on one of her visits). What sort of writing did I do, my grandmother wanted to know. For her, husband and children had always come first—how did modern girls manage career, husband, and children? In her silk *chuba* dress and turquoise jewelry, hair braided and coiled atop her head in the style she'd worn since the 1930s, she ruminated and reminisced about her battles with her unkind stepmother; the traditional marriage proposals she refused, too independent to "worship the he-man"; my great-grandfather riding his pony over 17,000-foot passes in the dead of winter to mediate a political dispute in Lhasa; Tibetan citizens who, after the 1959 uprising against the occupying Chinese, were "dragged round and round, whipped to death, put in the black cellar as punishment." And my mother, who, when leaving for America, "didn't shed one tear," just waved goodbye to her weeping parents and said, "Don't worry, I'll be perfectly all right."

On my visits to Darjeeling with my mother, the conversation would start out free-ranging and relaxed—one of the rare moments when the strain between my mother and grandmother abated. Though my mother had idolized her father, she harbored resentment toward her mother. She was amused by my grandmother's stories, which generally involved someone meeting a wretched end, but the mood changed when, inevitably, my grandmother told my mother to sort out the altar room or organize the photo albums before returning to California. (Thrilled that her granddaughter would journey for days to come see her, my grandmother was disinclined to order me around.) My mother hated how girls were expected first and foremost to be "good housegirls," regardless of their intelligence or achievements. She'd attempt to explain or negotiate, or just start shouting—*Even though I'm a doctor, you think all I'm good for is tidying the house!*—as my grandmother fell silent, expecting filial piety.

When my mother was growing up, she told me after one of these quarrels, girls who were too "bold" were "squelched." Then I better understood why she'd been so happy to go away to America. I also glimpsed something that would take time to fully grasp: both my grandmother and mother were iron-willed, independent women who'd supported their daughters' ambitions yet held to old-style expectations for girls. I came to see I could break the pattern with my own daughter. At the same time, I realized I'd inherited my determination from my grandmother and mother. I sensed myself being drawn in and reconnected, felt lines extending to the future.

In the ritual of tea—the lush aroma of the leaves grown in Darjeeling soil and the gleam of the silver tea service, the delicate weight of the Wedgwood china and the sound of tea being poured, the

> Then I better understood why she'd been so happy to go away to America.

flow of stories and conversation under the gaze of the heaven and hell gods on the *thangkas*—I've found what I traveled halfway around the world in search of after college. The taste of the tea varies, different notes coming to the fore—mellow or spicy, flowery or bitter—but the steady continuity of the ritual never wavers.

4.

From when I was a girl until I was in my early thirties, I had a recurring dream about trying to run away though my legs were filled with wet sand. I never dream this anymore.

At home in Tokyo, I enjoy my tea surrounded by *thangkas*, the traditional blue-and-white porcelain teacups with silver lids that were a wedding present from my grandmother, a prayer wheel from the family altar room. Until my grandmother died in 2004,

my children loved having tea with her at Annandale, eating prodigious amounts of *gram* and cake while listening to her stories and answering her questions about their lives. On the last day of our visit, my grandmother would take us to the prayer room and touch our foreheads to the altar. Generations of our family prayed in that room; it was where my mother said the old Tibetan prayers as a girl. Next to the flickering butter lamps and statues of deities was a battered copper *gau* locket that family members had worn for protection on journeys. I always wanted to tell my children that times had changed, that their paths would be easier than my mother's and mine. Instead, I'd help them light incense as an offering to the ancestors and the gods. Then my grandmother would walk me and the children to the car, wish us happy landings, and give us big packets of tea to take home. ◈

Tea

REQUIRED:

High-quality tea from a Darjeeling estate (whole leaf, small size)

METHOD:

1. Fill a clean teapot, silver if you are entertaining, with hot water to pre-warm.

2. Heat cold spring water over a strong fire to a rolling boil. Empty the teapot and put in one teaspoon of loose tea leaves for each person and "one for the pot." Pour in the boiling water.

3. Allow the leaves to remain loose in the water. The idea is to let them expand fully and steep until a nice brown color sets in.

4. After infusing the leaves for about four minutes, pour piping hot through a strainer (stainless steel, to avoid a metallic taste) into Wedgwood or other lovely china cups. Enjoy with sugar and warmed milk from a creamer, both with lace covers to keep off flies.

NOTES:

1. Foods of strong as well as dainty taste draw out the intricate notes of the tea. On the table there should be the following: finger sandwiches such as cheese-chutney and egg-watercress, and special homemade confectionery that may include scones with clotted cream and jam, rock buns (fruit cakes), Victoria sponge cake, Eccles cake (buttery round pastry with currants), etc. If you like, include one bowl of spicy *gram*.

2. A quantity of fresh flowers from the garden may be spread round the table.

3. For special guests, items kept under lock and key by the mistress of the house may be taken out, viz. American peanut butter and English chocolates.

4. Never hesitate to enjoy one drop of sherry at tea, particularly when your guests are dull or you are in receipt of troubling news.

5. You must not lift the saucer together with the cup when drinking, or blow on the tea to cool it. Finger sandwiches, though small, are not to be put in the mouth at one go. Exercise care not to talk too much. (n.b. These rules may be set aside in the case of children.)

David Baker is poetry editor of the *Kenyon Review*. His latest book of poems is *Scavenger Loop*.

Rick Barot's most recent book of poems is *Chord*, which received the UNT Rilke Prize and the PEN Open Book Award.

Curtis Bauer's recent work has appeared in the *Offing*, *American Poetry Review*, *Tupelo Quarterly*, and *World Literature Today*. He teaches at Texas Tech University.

Craig Beaven lives with his wife and children in Tallahassee, Florida. His poems are out in *Best New Poets 2016*, *Pleiades*, *Quarterly West*, and elsewhere.

Elizabeth Bradfield runs Broadsided Press, works as a naturalist, and teaches at Brandeis University. Her most recent poetry collection is *Once Removed*.

Chris Carroll's writing has appeared in the *New York Review of Books*, *Lapham's Quarterly*, the *Wall Street Journal*, and elsewhere.

Abigail Chabitnoy's poems have appeared in *Hayden's Ferry Review*, *Pleiades*, *Tinderbox Poetry Journal*, *Nat. Brut*, *Red Ink*, *Mud City*, and *Permafrost*. She lives in Colorado.

Chen Chen is the author of *When I Grow Up I Want to Be a List of Further Possibilities*.

Cassandra Cleghorn is a poet from California who lives in Vermont and teaches in Massachusetts. Her book, *Four Weathercocks*, came out in 2016.

Megan Fernandes lives in NYC. Her work is published in *Rattle*, *Guernica*, *Pank*, *Thrush*, *Denver Quarterly*, etc. She is an assistant professor at Lafayette College.

John Fischer is a writer currently living in Brooklyn. His essays have appeared in the *Atlantic*, *Guernica*, the *Sun*, and elsewhere.

Joseph Frankel is an essayist, journalist, and fiction writer based in New York City. His work has also appeared in the *Atlantic*.

Seth Fried's stories have appeared in numerous publications. He is the winner of two Pushcart Prizes and the author of a short story collection, *The Great Frustration*.

Ginger Gaffney writes and trains horses in New Mexico. Other chapters from this book appear in *Witness*, *Utne Reader*, and *Quarterly West*.

Lauren Haldeman is the author of *Instead of Dying*, winner of the 2017 Colorado Prize for Poetry, and *Calenday*.

Marcus Jackson teaches in the MFA program at Ohio State, and his second collection of poems, *Pardon My Heart*, will be released in 2018.

Tania James is the author of *Atlas of Unknowns*, *Aerogrammes*, and *The Tusk That Did the Damage*.

Taylor Johnson is proud of being from Washington, DC. Their work appears in or is forthcoming from *Callaloo*, the *Shade Journal*, *Third Coast*, and *BOAAT*.

John Koethe's most recent book is *The Swimmer*. *Walking Backwards: Poems 1966 – 2016* will be published in 2018.

Ada Limón is the author of four books, including *Bright Dead Things*, which was named a finalist for the National Book Award in Poetry.

Rohan Maitzen is a literary critic, an editor, and an English professor; she lives in Halifax, Nova Scotia.

Kseniya Melnik's debut book is the story collection *Snow in May*. Born in Russia, she moved to Alaska in 1998, and resides in Los Angeles.

Delaney Nolan's fiction has appeared in *Electric Literature*, *Guernica*, *Oxford American*, and elsewhere. She is currently a Fulbright fellow in Bulgaria.

Carl Phillips teaches at Washington University in St. Louis. His most recent book of poems is *Wild Is the Wind*.

Paisley Rekdal is the author, most recently, of *Imaginary Vessels* and *The Broken Country*.

Natalie Scenters-Zapico is the author of *The Verging Cities* and *Lima :: Limón*.

Matthew Siegel is the author of *Blood Work*. He teaches literature and writing at San Francisco Conservatory of Music.

Ann Tashi Slater's work has been published by the *New Yorker*, the *Paris Review*, and *Granta* en español, among others. She lives in Tokyo. www.anntashislater.com.

Sofi Stambo has been published in *Guernica*, *Agni*, *American Short Fiction*, the *Kenyon Review*, *New England Review*, *Stand*, and elsewhere.

Mark Steinmetz lives and works in Athens, Georgia. He has made over a dozen photography books, most with Nazraeli Press.

Bianca Stone is a poet and visual artist. She runs the Ruth Stone Foundation, and her new book, *The Möbius Strip Club of Grief*, is forthcoming.

Ross White is the director of Bull City Press and the author of two chapbooks, *The Polite Society* and *How We Came Upon the Colony*.

Leni Zumas is the author of three books of fiction: *Red Clocks*, *The Listeners*, and *Farewell Navigator*. She teaches writing at Portland State University.

FRONT COVER:
Ski Holidays, Photoshop, 8 ½″ x 11″, 2014 © Ryo Takemasa.
www.ryotakemasa.com.

CREDITS:
Page 141: Photographs from *Angel City West* are reprinted courtesy of Charles A. Hartman Fine Art, Portland, Oregon.

STATEMENT OF OWNERSHIP
and circulation for Tin House

Statement of ownership and circulation for Tin House, pub. no. 1542-521. Filed September 30, 2017. Published quarterly, x4 issues annually: Spring, Summer, Fall, and Winter. Annual subscription price $50.00. General business office and headquarters: McCormack Communications LLC, 2601 NW Thurman St, Portland OR 97210-2202. Publisher: Win McCormack, c/o McCormack Communications LLC, 2601 NW Thurman St, Portland, OR 97210-2202. Editor: Rob Spillman, c/o McCormack Communications LLC, 2601 NW Thurman St, Portland OR 97210-2202. Managing editor: Cheston Knapp, c/o McCormack Communications LLC, 2601 NW Thurman St, Portland OR 97210-2202. Owner: Win McCormack, c/o McCormack Communications LLC, 2601 NW Thurman St, Portland OR 97210-2202. There are no other bondholders, mortgagees or other holders. Extent and nature of circulation: net press run average copies per issue during preceding 12 months: 10,547 actual copies single issue, nearest filing date: 10,600; paid and/or requested circulation average copies per issue during 12 preceding months: 6,377; actual copies single issue nearest filing date: 5,689; mail subscription average copies per issue during preceding 12 months: 4,381; actual copies single issue nearest filing date: 4,009; total paid and/or requested circulation through vendors average copies per issue during the 12 months: 1,997; actual copies single issue nearest filing date: 1,680; free distribution by mail average copies per issue during preceding 12 months: 378; actual copies single issue nearest filing date: 404; total free distribution average copies per issue during preceding 12 months: 378; actual copies single issue nearest filing date: 404; total distribution: average copies per issue during preceding 12 months: 6,755; actual copies single issue nearest filing date: 6,093; copies not distributed average copies per issue during preceding 12 months: 3,792; actual copies single issue nearest filing date: 4,507; total average copies per issue nearest filing date: 10,547 actual copies single issue nearest filing date: 10,600. Percent paid and/or requested circulation during preceding 12 months: 94.40%; nearest to filing date: 93.40%. Paid electronic copies per issue during preceding 12 months: 180, paid electronic copies single issue nearest filing date: 155; total print and paid copies during preceding 12 months: 6,557; total paid print and electronic copies single issue nearest filing date: 6,248; total print distribution and paid electronic copies during preceding 12 months: 6,935; total print distribution and paid electronic copies single issue nearest filing date: 6,248. Percent paid and/or requested circulation (print and electronic copies) during preceding 12 months: 94.50%; percent paid and/or requested circulation (print and electronic copies) single issue nearest filing date: 93.5%. Tin House certifies the above statements are correct and complete.

Printed by Versa Press.

WE KNOW IT'S BEEN A LONG HIATUS, AND WE KNOW
IT MAY TAKE A WHILE FOR THIS TO SINK IN, BUT:

THE BELIEVER IS BACK. >

**STARTING WITH OUR AUGUST/SEPTEMBER '17 ISSUE, WE WILL
PUBLISH BI-MONTHLY FROM OUR NEW HOME IN** *LAS VEGAS, NEVADA.*

We're going to bring you special issues, new columns, and bonus material, and we will do this all while wearing an old pair of Tevas because it's straight up too hot to wear shoes down here and we lost our flip-flops during the move.

Please read. Please subscribe. And come visit. Our new headquarters is the Beverly Rogers, Carol C. Harter Black Mountain Institute, an international literary center at UNLV. The best time to see us would be the spring, when the neon is blooming, and when we'll be hosting our annual festival for the magazine. We kicked things off in the spring of '17 with **Miranda July, Dave Eggers, Luís Alberto Urrea, Sally Wen Mao,** *and many others. Everyone had a lot of fun and talked about books and American Dreams; we can't wait to do it over and over again. Please join our mailing list at believermag.com. And if you haven't already, will you subscribe? You won't regret it. There are a lot of good things on the horizon.*

Yours, { BLACKMOUNTAININSTITUTE.ORG
BELIEVERMAG.COM

MFA
CREATIVE WRITING
FICTION – POETRY

TEXAS ★ STATE
UNIVERSITY®
The rising STAR of Texas

Our campus overlooks the scenic Hill Country town of San Marcos, part of the Austin Metropolitan Area. With Austin just 30 miles to the north, Texas State students have abundant opportunities to enjoy music, dining, outdoor recreation, and more.

Tim O'Brien
Professor of Creative Writing

Naomi Shihab Nye
Visiting Professor 2017-18

Karen Russell
Endowed Chair 2017-19

Faculty

Fiction
Doug Dorst
Jennifer duBois
Tom Grimes
Debra Monroe

Poetry
Cyrus Cassells
Roger Jones
Cecily Parks
Kathleen Peirce
Steve Wilson

Visiting Writers*
Gabrielle Calvocoressi
Lydia Davis
Junot Díaz
Stephen Dunn
Stuart Dybek
Martín Espada
Ross Gay
Jorie Graham
Lauren Groff
Terrance Hayes
Marlon James
Leslie Jamison
Adam Johnson
Ada Limón
Philipp Meyer
Mary Ruefle
Tracy K. Smith
Ocean Vuong

Adjunct Thesis Faculty
Lee K. Abbott
Gina Apostol
Catherine Barnett
Rick Bass
Kevin Brockmeier
Gabrielle Calvocoressi
Ron Carlson
Victoria Chang
Maxine Chernoff
Joanna Klink
Eduardo Corral
Charles D'Ambrosio
Natalie Diaz
John Dufresne
Carolyn Forché
James Galvin
Amelia Gray
Saskia Hamilton
Amy Hempel
Bret Anthony Johnston

T. Geronimo Johnson
Li-Young Lee
Karan Mahajan
Nina McConigley
Elizabeth McCracken
Jane Mead
Mihaela Moscaliuc
David Mura
Kirstin Valdez Quade
Spencer Reece
Alberto Ríos
Elissa Schappell
Richard Siken
Gerald Stern
Natalia Sylvester
Justin Torres
Brian Turner
Eleanor Wilner
Monica Youn

* Recent and upcoming

Now offering courses in creative nonfiction.

$70,000 Scholarship:
W. Morgan and Lou Claire Rose Fellowship for an incoming student. Additional scholarships and teaching assistantships available.

Front Porch, our literary journal:
frontporchjournal.com

Doug Dorst, MFA Director
Department of English

601 University Drive
San Marcos, TX 78666-4684
512.245.7681

Tin House Magazine

Save 50% off the newsstand price

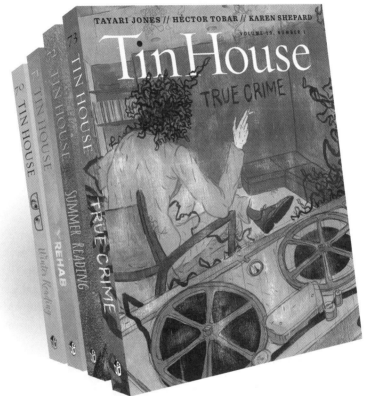

Subscribe today, only $34.95

Missed the first 73 issues?

Fear not, we've hidden a limited number in our closet.
Log on to www.tinhouse.com for more information.

ABOUT THE COVER

In *Ski Holidays*, Ryo Takemasa contrasts a quiet covering of snow with the vibrant warmth of the sun. A sentry-like deer complements the slice of skis. The overall sense is that of a fleeting moment. Takemasa's work is often location and time specific. He pairs movement—falling rain, a rush of commuters, a luggage-laden car traveling down a hillside—with the stillness of landscape and architecture to evoke not just a sense of place "but the sense of a certain place at a certain time."

Takemasa has used various techniques over the years, from watercolor to woodcut to manga. He discovered his current style in college and has continued to develop it ever since. He was inspired to pursue illustration when he learned about the graphic designer and optical illusionist Shigeo Fukuda. Takemasa's work is also greatly influenced by his favorite illustrator, Ryohei Yanagihara, a key figure in Japanese animation of the 1960s who was known for his angular, pink-hued figures.

Though he works digitally, Takemasa's illustrations have a handmade aesthetic, like that of traditional printmaking. His crisp shapes and color overlays look as if they could have been screen printed. The soft textures have a vintage feel. Exaggerated angles lend a cinematic tone, giving his work a unique perspective.

You can see more of Takemasa's art at www.ryotakemasa.com

Written by *Tin House* designer Jakob Vala, based on an interview with the artist.